As Joan Approaches Infinity

As Joan Approaches Infinity

Kika Dorsey

Gesture Press
Denver, CO

Gesture Press
Denver, CO
gesturepressandjournal.com

ISBN: 979-8-9873231-0-6
Cataloging in-publication data is available from the Library of Congress

First Edition | First Printing
Printed in the United States of America

To Michael, Sam, and Eliza

I Have Been Her Kind:
A Foreword

Sarah Elizabeth Schantz

After finishing Kika Dorsey's incredible debut in fiction, I couldn't help but liken the character of Joan to the Chimera oracle card created by Nitasia Roland[1]. Roland describes Chimera as "a mythic hybrid creature of strength and cunning, [that] … represents a … connection with wild feminine energy, an archetype of the transgressive, the trickster, the tempter," and just as Chimera "is both attractive and repulsive," so is Joan because she pushes the boundaries that attempt to limit her earthly (and potentially finite) experience.

Whether it's literature or film, I've long had an affinity for the lonely, often violent narratives that unfold from the picket fence settings of white-flight manufactured suburbia. This fascination is likely rooted in the fact that this is not a world I know well; there is something inherently disturbing about these landscapes where fictitious wives Stepford themselves and all-too-real white kids shoot up their schools. I can't seem to look away from these neighborhoods governed by the social rating system of Next Door, these cookie cutter homes where middle-to-upper-middleclass America has decided to "safely" raise its children.

I think I'm looking for the malignant tumor that leeches out into the rest of society so I might know how to cut it away, and thus I've devoured the fiction of John Cheever, John Irving, Tom Perrotta, and Jeffrey Eugenides, but as a woman approaching fifty I've grown tired

---

[1] The Chimera card is from the Chimera Tarot Deck created by Natasia Roland.

of such stories always being centered on the male protagonists, their midlife crises the predictable plotlines (receding hairlines, Viagra, shiny new cars, fellatio from the babysitter, and divorce). So I was delighted to meet Joan, especially as she declares herself to be Jesus in the very first line!

Like all of us, Joan is a victim of the human condition; she expects to emerge from disaster enlightened only to find herself more exhausted than she already was. As Joan approaches infinity, she does so in a minivan while coasting toward an "empty nest" and the knowledge her "sunset years" are on the horizon further magnified by her mother's dementia; she maneuvers the speed bumps of her life, and as her author, Dorsey never shies away from the ugly. When we bear witness to Joan's attempts to accept her grossly underpaid position as an adjunct English professor or navigate the minefield that is her ever-critical, hickey-covered, eye-rolling teenage daughter, we can relate; we understand how these less-than-satisfactory moments are infectious, prone to blooming into a cruel monotony where death soon becomes the only tangible escape. Yet, Joan is more bewildered than she is disenchanted (if not mortified and enraged); still full of spirit, desire, and passion, Joan emerges from the page, asking herself, "Well, how did I get here?"[2]

Yes, Joan is flawed and absolutely self-absorbed (certain readers might even label her a "Karen"), but at least she's still asking this question. Joan is at a stage in life where most people in our late-stage capitalist grind just surrender, but rather than feeding the knife-hurt of her identity crisis to a white noise machine of antidepressants, benzos, Netflix, and whatever other dulling agents most Americans turn to, Joan is not only looking at her reflection in the steel blade, she is testing the sharpness of its edge to see if she still bleeds.

Besides, it's precisely these "unlikeable" traits that made me fall in love with Joan. I might not be your typical housewife or mother, but I

---

[2] Cue The Talking Heads' song "Once in a Lifetime" from the 1980 album, *Remain in Light*.

can say this: while I contain multitudes as a human being, the fact I am a mother has forced me to conform to mainstream society more than I ever thought I would, and I did so to protect my daughters from what might happen to them if I didn't. This is a sacrifice Joan makes for her kids as well, but they never once thank her. Therefore I'm eternally grateful to Joan who becomes my alter ego as she should yours; for women like me, Joan is our savior—when she acts out, we get to do so vicariously—in her performance of the taboo, Joan becomes an outlet for our rage.

I've taught enough creative writing workshops to anticipate what many readers, especially men, are bound to say about Joan. Because I've heard the same labels used for other "unlikeable" women written by other women writers, I predict they will accuse her of being self-involved, impulsive, reckless, over-indulgent, narcissistic, and even dangerous. Joan is neither the perfect mother nor the ideal whore, and this alone is her gravest sin. Joan serves time in jail, drinks way too much, steals and cheats, and yet she (almost) always gets dinner on the table, is the sole caregiver for her dying mother, and a lover and rescuer of animals (albeit a slightly irresponsible pet owner, her heart is in the right place, and sometimes that is what matters most).

Joan has far more redeeming qualities than J.D. Salinger's entitled, yet still (somehow) beloved, not-so-golden boy, Holden Caulfield. And Joan is definitely a better person than Vladimir Nabokov's middle-aged pedophile will ever be—Humbert Humbert's redundant name only further evidence of his narcissism. And Joan is certainly a saint when compared to Patrick Bateman, Bret Easton Ellis' deeply misogynistic "*American Psycho.*"

According to Biblio.com, *The Catcher in the Rye* has sold more than 65 million copies since 1951 when it was first published with a $3.00 price sticker; Salinger's bildungsroman has been widely banned for profanity, sexual conduct, and its portrayal of teenage angst since its inception, and yet it is lauded as one of the great American novels, a bible for surviving puberty—that is, if you're a whiny white boy burdened by the expectations of an Ivy League trajectory and a future New York City apartment adjacent to Central Park.[3]

Lolita was also written and published in the 1950s, and like *The Catcher in the Rye*, it was considered scandalous at the time, censored both in France where it debuted, and then the United States, the United Kingdom, and so forth. However, and I loudly clear my throat as I say this, people—especially men—have always fought for its literary merit (just as they have waged wars in honor of *The Catcher in the Rye* and *American Psycho*). *Lolita* has been adapted to film twice (first by Stanley Kubrick in 1962, then by Adrian Lyne in 1997), and to the stage several times (including opera, ballet, and even a Broadway musical), and remains (rightfully) listed amidst the top 100 best novels of all time; the story is so embedded in our culture, we see references to it everywhere: in the song "Off to the Races," a millennial-aged Lana Del Rey uses a girlish voice and demeanor to deliver the lyrics, "Light of my life, fire of my loins"[4]; she sings the persona of a young woman whose "old man is a bad man," a sugar daddy "thief" who is also her "one true love"; meanwhile, "Humbert" appears in the Urban Dictionary as slang for "an adult (usually male) who harbors and/or expresses ~~inappropriate~~[5] affections for a minor."

And then there's this outrageously fun fact regarding *American Psycho*: the book was originally slated to be published by Simon & Schuster, but when controversy was already mounting just over the anticipation of the not-yet-released novel, one month before scheduled publication, Simon & Schuster reneged; but more to the point, while they refused to ever publish the book, they told the author he could still keep the

---

[3] Interestingly enough it seems even Salinger tired of poor Holden as his character appears in some of the author's short stories as missing in action during World War II even though the timelines make this impossible suggesting he wanted to get rid of the kid once and for all.

[4] The infamous opening of Nabokov's *Lolita*.

[5] "Inappropriate" should be replaced by "illegal" or "criminal." Is this "soft language"? If so, does it then reflect a residual acceptance that it's perfectly normal for men (adults) to fetishize girls (children)?

$300,000 advance he'd already received.[6] (Does white male privilege not get any more blatant than this?!? Especially in a world where women writers rarely see six-figure advances for the books their publishers do publish?). In his article, "The Savage Ethics of 'American Psycho,'" John Paul Rollert passionately (and accurately) declares Ellis' novel to be "the single most damning critique of the cultural consequences of contemporary capitalism." Joining the fandom, Irvine Welsh also applauds Ellis' third novel in a review published by The Guardian writes: "American Psycho holds a hyper-real, satirical mirror up to our faces, and the uncomfortable shock of recognition it produces is that twisted reflection of ourselves, and the world we live in …"

I am not condemning *American Psycho, Lolita,* or *The Catcher in the Rye,* but I am criticizing a double standard we cannot ignore: why are readers so quick to dismiss unlikeable female characters written by women when unlikeable characters of any gender written by men receive such a literary circle-jerk of praise?

To return to Roland's description of the Chimera, and the magnetic idea of such a creature being both "attractive" and "repulsive," I'd like to examine the tension of this push-pull as it relates to all the books I've discussed (including Dorsey's). First, let's uproot the word "allure" from the etymology of the adjective "attractive." The three iconic characters created by Salinger, Nabokov, and Ellis, all lure the reader in using the phenomena known as "The Call of the Void," those moments when we are beckoned to the edge of existence to look at the unattractive, whether it be evil, or death, or whatever else we fear or do not understand. Salinger, Nabokov, and Ellis employ skillfully crafted unreliable narrators as the lens through which we see. As a verb, "attract," especially its etymological roots within the realm of medicine (attracten), is a force that also "absorbs" and "draws out" (think bandage or poultice).

Art acts as a mirror through which we see ourselves reflected back,

---

[6] Vintage Books ended up publishing the book in 1991 (they are now an imprint of Penguin Random House).

the human condition, and all its contradictions, but characters like Humbert Humbert and Patrick Bateman are categorical antiheros who provide a particular service; they personify the antagonistic culture which oppresses us all, and in their specific cases, they are working allegories for the evils of the patriarchy and late-stage capitalism. They are repulsive because they are predators; we are not supposed to identify with them because we are their victims.

Joan, on the other hand, is flawed. She is more akin to Holden Caulfield[7], yet unlike Joan, Holden gets to grow up to be a white man from money, the crème de la crème, whereas Joan (however white and middleclass[8]), will always be a woman, and women are inherently unlikeable because the dominant mythology says so; she has been unlikeable since she first appeared in literature, naked in a garden, plucking an apple from a tree; she's been detested for centuries ever-after for wanting (and taking) more, so no, I'm not ashamed to confess my attraction to the disaster of her character. In Joan I recognize my own rage and I am attracted to what it can apparently do; as Anne Sexton wrote, "I have been her kind."[9]

In "The Laugh of the Medusa," Hélène Cixous asks the question: "What woman hasn't flown/stolen? Who hasn't felt, dreamt, performed the gesture that jams sociality?" Cixous continues: "A feminine text cannot fail to be more than subversive. It is volcanic; as it is written it brings about an upheaval of the old property crust, carrier of masculine investments; there's no other way. There's no room for her if she's not

---

[7] I've been unfair to Holden; the truth is I love J.D. Salinger's short stories, and it's been so long since I read *The Catcher in the Rye* I don't actually know how I might feel about it now; furthermore, I see how devotees of Holden identify with him because Salinger's portrayal of P.T.S.D., depression, and grief are so accurate (I think of "A Perfect Day for Bananafish" which I *have* read recently, and there is no denying the work Salinger did to raise a much-needed mental health awareness, especially for boys who are raised not to talk about their feelings.

[8] Middleclass in today's America, especially given the series of unfortunate events Joan faces in the novel, should be understood as only one catastrophe away from potential destitution.

[9] From the poem, "Her Kind."

a he. If she's a her-she, it's in order to smash everything, to shatter the framework of institutions, to blow fail to be more than subversive. It is volcanic; as it is written it brings about an upheaval of the old property crust, carrier of masculine investments; there's no other way. There's no room for her if she's not a he. If she's a her-she, it's in order to smash everything, to shatter the framework of institutions, to blow up the law, to break up the 'truth' with laughter." Cixous might as well have been describing As Joan Approaches Infinity (even though her theory far precedes Dorsey's novel), and as I marveled over this correspondence between the two texts, the synapses began to fire.

Right now I am working on a book I've been warned not to write, another forbidden fruit that might topple all of paradise if I so dare to pick it from The Tree of Knowledge. Like Dorsey's book, this novel I'm writing is dripping with dark humor; in general, I am concerned about such narratives because they're an endangered species given the fact critical thinking is all but extinct, especially the ability to decipher nuance or irony, but the true epiphany I had was this: women aren't allowed to write satire.

I think of Medusa's laughter, and I realize what makes certain readers so uncomfortable when they read As Joan Approaches Infinity is just how hilarious Dorsey's book really is, and that's when I finally got it; the readers who will squirm the most are the ones who know the joke's on them. The rest of us will be laughing with Joan all the way to The End (and ever after into infinity).

Holden Caulfield, Humbert Humbert, and Patrick Bateman are all delivered to us via first-person whereas Dorsey's unreliable narration is third-person limited omniscience. As someone who's followed the evolution of this novel from its genesis, I've contemplated (and even questioned) Dorsey's choice. At first I worried her choice was influenced, perhaps subconsciously, by the criticism she had to know she'd be up against for writing a "Karen."[10] Did she fear people would mistake her fiction as memoir? Mix her up with Joan? I thought back to early in my career, and the series of rejection letters I received from six different male editors at six different journals—back then, before electronic submissions (and the invention of the wheel), to save money and paper, publications would print four rejection letters to one sheet of paper, then cut them into slips, and mail these back in SASEs you provided. I received these same slips when I was rejected by these publications, only the male editors had taken the time to also write to me by hand, scrawled attempts at mansplaining where they told me they didn't publish creative nonfiction or memoir. However, they'd failed at the mansplaining part because I knew this already, because I had submitted fiction (granted, my short stories were first-person). And if you think I am exaggerating, then why do so many of my students mistake female authors as their first-person female characters (especially if the characters are sexy or "unlikeable")?

If Ellis had no qualms forcing his readers to inhabit the mind of a yuppie serial killer—to make us embody Bateman as he commits such gruesome acts of violence—one would think it'd be no big deal to read Joan as Joan herself. But then I realized this was one of the ways Dorsey was not only distinguishing her work as satire, but as a parable too (after all, Dorsey's protagonist does indeed share a name with a certain misunderstood female saint). I believe Dorsey knows the world is watching women like Joan, waiting for "her" to fall, for her to fail; they are waiting to pounce on her disgrace, to call her out and cancel her, thus Dorsey's perspective allows the reader to maintain such a voyeuristic stance to then be eclipsed by the intimacy her very close third-person narration provides.

Furthermore, Joan has reached the age where women become

---

[10] I call Joan a "Karen" both as a joke and a reality; she is "both/and." Moreover, if Patrick Bateman is a personification of capitalist greed and consumer gluttony, and *American Psycho* serves as a mirror we need to look at because as a society we are complicit in the making of this monster, I think we can handle looking at the "Karen" archetype and considering the implications of her as a cultural zeitgeist.

invisible. By writing Joan in third-person, Dorsey is making the reader look, but by choosing third-person limited she is also making them experience Joan's interiority. The so-called literary canon is steeped in testosterone-drenched stories that surf this hormonal tide all the way from puberty to impotence, gifting the world a cast of male characters who range a vast spectrum from toxic to tender; and while the canon does include several coming-of-age tales that feature girls or young women, and pregnancy is a common go-to countdown plot strategy, a woman in menopause is apparently prohibited, and this is why Dorsey's novel is not only a social critique on sexism but a story that examines sexism as compounded by ageism.

One of the many unfortunate side effects of the patriarchy is our tendency to overlook our shadow anima in favor of our shadow animus. Dorsey has crafted a clever parable by creating Joan. She uses selfishness, the absolute no-no for women of any age, as the only successful way Joan ever manages to liberate herself, however temporarily, from the tedium of domestic life and an existence where women were born to be blamed. Through her absorption in self, Joan refuses to vanish just because the male gaze no longer looks her way. With her sarcastic wit, Dorsey has resurrected the sharp tongue of Dorothy Parker by daring to write a satire, a genre still dominated by male writers and male characters, and by doing so she has joined rank with the likes of A.M. Homes and Mary Gaitskill.

I'm thrilled to see this book edited and published by the likes of Heather Goodrich, and the feminist gestures of her press. I believe this laugh-out-loud dark comedy Dorsey and Joan have dished out for us will serve to save us from the virtue-signaling facades and personas that stifle and pervert us all. Like the poet CA Conrad once told me, "Anything forced into a closet can only fester."

As Joan Approaches Infinity

The Savior

After the universe gave her multiple hints, Joan finally realized that she was Jesus Christ. Her children, Jeremy and Michele, and husband, Darren, blamed her for everything—lost backpacks because they were sure they set it on the kitchen counter, and she must have cleaned it up. It was her fault when they were late for school, even though they were the ones fumbling about in the house while she sat in the car waiting. She was "mean" when she asked about their grades, and what was she thinking when she didn't have an auto insurance document filed (because she apparently was the one to keep track of paperwork). She was certainly taking on the sins of the world.

She'd had a dream. In the dream she was sitting with an audience, and on the stage was a Buddha wearing an orange robe and sitting cross-legged. He was humming "Om," and somehow Joan knew that if she joined him, she would feel all the pain in the world and die.

She figured Jesus and Buddha were the same person, even though Jesus was usually depicted as white with long brown hair and a brown robe and preferred eating last suppers to meditating. Also, when her father committed suicide by flying head-first out of the second-floor window of the homeless shelter, he'd left a note that he would return to Christ.

And he'd returned to Joan in dreams and in her daily life because he had basically bailed on her dear demented mother, and Joan felt like she was being nailed to a cross when she had to become her mother's caretaker, which then led her to become a drunk and landed her in jail, where her apostles complained about the watery beans, and in general were quite unpleasant to her. They'd roll their eyes when she talked about her troubles, even though she praised their tattoos. One woman named Dawn had a tattoo of Jesus on the cross, the red ink of blood dripping from her forearm onto her inner wrist, and Joan even then knew that image was like a mirror: her blood, her pain.

Then again, maybe she was just hung-over.

That day of her arrest had been an especially grueling day of taking on other people's sins. Jeremy had broken the first commandment by killing a spider in his room; then Michele lied to her about the bottle of wine in her closet; both her children were not honoring their mother and father; and her husband was lusting after their neighbor Spencer's wife, Kate (a commandment that often confused her, because wasn't Kate a neighbor too?), and he was coveting their new truck.

Joan had just finished swimming after visiting the Social Security office for the tenth time to try to get Medicare for the woman who'd birthed her and changed her diapers, whose own diapers now needed to be changed because Joan's mother didn't always remember that she had a body still. Joan smelled like chlorine and carried with her the womblike embrace of the water that always helped pull her through the day. She was in the kitchen sneaking gulps of tequila and then thought what the hell, and poured herself a martini. Her stomach was empty, and instead of eating lunch, she poured another shot in her glass and drank it.

When she drove to the grocery store to buy chicken and pasta for dinner, she sideswiped a green Subaru, and when the cops came, she resisted arrest and kicked one of them in the shin.

"You have the right to remain silent—"

"I'm sick of being silent!" Joan said before he had the chance to finish reading her rights. "I have a lot to say."

In a tired voice, he finished his reading of the rights and said, "I will have to charge you with assaulting a police officer."

Joan slumped in the back of the police car, shackled and lonely, her wrists hurting, her mind spinning. Who would pick up the kids for the orthodontist appointment? The office already charged an arm and leg for the braces both Michele and Jeremy now wore, but the cancellation fees were just as handsome. And what if the braces that needed to be tightened got loose and then they'd have to start over and the $3,476.32 they'd already spent on their winning smiles doubled as a result?

When Darren bailed her out the next day, Joan swore she smelled Kate on him, the odor of lemon balm from a salve Kate used on her sore muscles after doing weights for two hours every other day. Darren kissed Joan on the cheek and said little. He frowned as he drove. Joan wondered how much he had paid to bail her out but didn't ask because she could tell he was angry. She did some deep-breathing exercises and thought of what her therapist once told her, to focus on the positive, to not plunge into the abyss of self-loathing and fear.

She had shed herself of the orange jumpsuit two sizes too big for her, put in her nose stud and slid her rings on her fingers—her wedding ring, the garnet ring from her mother, the ring from her husband with all the birth stones of her family. Hers was aquamarine blue like the pools where she swam while somewhere someone learned how to walk on water. But she didn't need to because she was a good swimmer, and she would swim through a pool of tears all the way to heaven.

That's what Jesus did.

Killing or Taking Care of the Living

Sobriety was overrated. Joan had to quit drinking because of her DUI, and every morning she had to call probation, punch in eight numbers, 19605493, she now knew by heart, and find out if she would be tested that day. Testing meant driving to Interventions and peeing in a cup with a temperature sticker on the side while a female probation officer watched. Since she couldn't drink or even smoke pot or she'd end up in jail again, she felt the same way all day and hardly slept. She did have a prescription for Valium, though, so she was allowed to occasionally relieve her panic attacks or insomnia.

Drinking had its advantages and disadvantages. It made her send emails she regretted or say things that offended people. She would come home from teaching composition at Mountain View Community College, where she taught adjunct, feeling enervated by her indifferent students. Then she would comfort herself from the mundanity of her life by sending out emails to all her friends living in different cities, telling them she missed them, lugubrious emails full of tears and pathos. Alyssa always called her back, her friend from college who now lived in L.A. But her other friends ignored her. Sometimes she saw Stephanie, but neither of them had much time for each other. Stephanie worked as a receptionist of a law firm, and Joan was overwhelmed with her responsibilities to her mother and children. Joan was lonely.

She would also regret conversations she had when drunk. Once when waiting on a blood test at the doctor's, Joan decided to pass the time by going to the restroom and shooting back a shot of tequila she had in her purse. When she returned to the waiting room, she ran into a woman she'd met years ago when her children were on the same cross-country team. The woman, whose name she'd forgotten, complained about the rent she now paid since the divorce, a number that would leave Joan destitute, so Joan replied, "Well, maybe you should have stayed married then if you can't afford it." The woman smirked and returned to reading her People magazine.

Then drinking landed her in jail for driving drunk and kicking a cop. It made for sloppy sex. However, she had experienced elation, slept well at night, and cooking dinner without booze was boring. The chicken just looked dead and slimy, and she couldn't tune out the slime while listening to Nirvana with a glass of wine.

One October day, a month after her arrest, after a night of staring at the red numbers of the clock and thinking about her mother in the Alzheimer's Unit in the nursing home, she tried to capture the remnants of a dream, where she lost her mom in Vienna. There were huge, white statues of muscular Poseidon and Lipizzaner horses everywhere. She woke up and got up to make coffee, but almost tripped on half a dead rabbit in the living room, its guts spilling pink and white on the black Oriental rug. Joan sighed. She put it in a plastic bag and threw it out. Damn cat. She loved Henry but the constant corpses were getting tiresome. She called probation. It was a test day. It was also a day when she had to do community service at the Goodwill. That evening she would review a vegan restaurant. She would also visit her anger management class taught by a dopey woman with huge tortoise-shell glasses, who made the class meditate and think of "love, serenity, and peace." Joan just wanted to punch her in the face.

Joan went to Intervention, a junky building with dirty blue carpet. She sat on the black plastic chair and tried to read a sign in Spanish about a local AA meeting. One older woman waiting to get tested had red, oozing eyes from tattooing eyeliner on them, her hair dyed orange, her fingernails painted blue. The eyes became infected, she said. She explained to Joan that both she and her daughter were on probation at the same time. "My daughter, she's a wild one," she said, wiping the tears streaming from her swollen eyes. Her daughter apparently had been so drunk that she drove off the road and slammed into a cop car as they were arresting someone else. "She was stoned, too," the woman said. "She thought the flashing lights looked cool, and she wanted to get a closer look."

Joan always enjoyed hearing other people's stories. It made her feel less alone. "I kicked a cop," she said.

"Oh, that's bad. That's a felony," said the woman.

"Yeah, my lawyer bargained it down, though." Joan had a wave of anxiety thinking of the $12,000 they paid the lawyer, but it had been worth it. Her sentencing was now a misdemeanor. "Also, it couldn't have hurt much. It was just a little kick. I didn't like him grabbing my arm and cuffing me."

The woman took out tissue and dabbed at her right eye, inflamed and surrounded by red spots. "Those cuffs hurt."

When Joan's name was called, she passed the main office with stars next to the probation officers' names, praising them for the amount of clients they kept and managed not to release. She peed in the cup for a woman in torn jeans who crossed her arms and made Joan perform the task while standing, which only the mean ones did.

She came home, kicked off her shoes, only to step on the head of a mouse on the kitchen floor. She was of course barefoot when she did. After wiping the blood off the carpet and the sole of her foot as best she could, she headed out to Goodwill.

She signed in, went into the back room where there were long tables and boxes on the floor, and sorted out clothes. She discarded the stained socks and underwear and read the T-shirts. The T-shirts were full of wisdom. A black one said, *If you don't have anything nice to say, say it sarcastically*, while another one read, *Good morning. I see the assassins have failed.* Yet another was *I make beer disappear. What's your superpower?* Joan read the slogans and thought deeply about the synchronicity of the universe and how it spoke to her about her drinking and anger issues. She decided to light a candle to God that evening.

Before she visited her mother, she came home to a pile of blue feathers and a beak in the entryway. That made for one less blue jay in their backyard. Sighing, she swept the corpse up and threw it away.

The nursing home, Into the Light, wasn't far from her house. It smelled like air freshener and urine, and the entire building had green carpet and paintings of mountains, trees, and sunrises on a beach. Joan found her mother seated at a table where several residents were drawing and coloring with crayons. Her mother was in a wheelchair, so doped up that she couldn't walk anymore. It was the price her mother paid for the times she became violent and started throwing shoes at the caretaker. It had landed her mother in a psych ward in Denver for two months before they figured out how to drug her into a zombie state. Now her mother dozed and drooled.

Her mother was Austrian, growing up in Leoben after the war. She married Joan's father after meeting him in Italy where she worked at a restaurant waiting tables. She had short, thin brown hair and a Roman nose and demeanor that was neither gentle nor measured. When Joan's father flew off the handle, her mother acted as if it were like the weather, a passing storm. Nothing seemed to phase her.

When they had moved to Vienna, her mother homesick for her country, Joan sent her cards and poetry. Joan had grown up in Chicago, and when her parents left, she was in college in Boulder. She had felt abandoned but tried to embrace the fact that her parents were now in Europe. They were happy there. They played cards with her uncles, went to concerts, and ate at restaurants that served Wiener Schnitzel and spaetzle. They brought Joan's sister, Angelika, to finish her last years of high school there. When her mother started showing signs of dementia, repeating herself on the phone and forgetting what they had done the day before, Joan checked in on them every week, and Angelika told Joan she was getting worried. But that was years ago, and now she was here, just a mile away from the house where Joan was trying to raise her two kids.

Joan kissed her mother's cheek, paper-thin and soft. She sat at the table and watched demented Dan draw a house with a red crayon. Its roof was a circle. She turned to her mother, who was wearing the pretty white silk blouse Joan had bought from Goodwill one day, when her job had been to return clothing from the dressing rooms to the racks.

For three years Joan had been managing her care. She spent one of those years hiring lawyers for immigration and guardianship, establishing Medicare, and paying off bills in Austria. She also took care to make sure her mother was supplied with classy clothes. Her mother had always been so cultured, so refined, and Joan longed to give her some of her dignity, even in small details. Joan painted her mother's nails and bought her pretty clothes. The one advantage to her mother not being able to stand or walk anymore was that she could wear these clothes again—silk blouses, linen pants. For two years she'd had to wear "adaptive clothing," jumpers embroidered with butterflies and flowers with a zipper on the back to keep her from peeing on the carpet.

"Mom, how are you?" Joan asked, leaning over and touching her mother's hand.

Her mother, trembling and hunched, didn't even look into her eyes.

"I brought you some soap. It has lavender in it." Joan held the soap under her mother's nose. "Smell it," she said.

Her mother turned her head away. Joan thought of the boxes of cheap wine in the fridge of the nursing home and how much it had helped her with these visits. The room offered a large picture window overlooking 28th street which was forever under road construction, including today. Joan watched a bulldozer lift its head, then lower down to take a monstrous bite of asphalt and steel wire. Pigeons lined the sill on the other side of the glass, huddled together, while inside Dolly Parton tried to sing about Jolene stealing her man, but the volume was too low to compete with the roar of the construction trucks. She shifted in her seat and felt angry, but she didn't know whom she was mad at.

When Joan was sixteen, she and her mother had gotten into a huge fight. Before she'd kicked the cop, it was the one other time in her life she had been violent. It was summer in Chicago, and they sat in the dining room while the mosquitoes came out and the sun set, shadows lengthening like the long, drawn-out days. The streets hummed with cars returning from work.

As they ate the schnitzel and salad, her ten-year-old sister, Angelika, pushed the green leaves to the side of the plate where she wouldn't touch them (which would lead to their mother lecturing her about how healthy vegetables are). "Joan," her mother said instead, "You need to babysit Angelika tonight."

Joan lifted her head from her plate. She looked at her mother, who was wearing blue eye shadow, face smooth with foundation, her hair curled. "No, I will not. I have plans."

"Yes, you will," her mother replied, "We have plans."

Joan felt the bile rise in her throat, thinking how unfair it was that she always had to take care of her sister while her mom partied. She had plans to go bowling with her boyfriend, Tom. "You cunt!" she said.

Her mother stood up. The light of the setting sun drew her shadow long across the table and onto the dark wood floors where it stretched enormous. She leaned forward then and slapped Joan in the face.

Joan's cheek burned, and she slapped her mother right back, and her hand then burned like her cheek. She picked up her glass of lemonade, the dining room floor, stained dark like her mother's eyes piercing at her, her father looking at them with blank eyes and saying nothing. Joan poured her drink over her mother's head. Her mother clenched her fists, permed brown hair flattening and dripping. Joan stormed out of the house and stood by the maple tree in the front yard to collect herself. She looked across the street at the brick house with the Catholic family of six boys and watched one of them hit the other with a stick while the daughter climbed a tree. Their beagle was chained to a doghouse and barking.

That evening she returned to the house in time to babysit after all. While her mother quickly showered and changed her clothes, Joan called her boyfriend and asked him to come over. Tom arrived with chocolate ice cream about twenty minutes after her parents pulled away in their car. They played "Go Fish" with Angelika and watched an episode of Gilligan's Island. At 10:00, they tucked Angelika into bed and made out on the couch downstairs.

She and her mother never talked about what happened.

Joan wheeled her mother into her room and rubbed the special dry shampoo into her mother's greasy hair and brushed it in, the white powder enhancing the strands of silver. She set a picture on the desk her uncle had sent her of him, his flushed face smiling in the Vienna woods with the burst of green trees in the background. Her mother loved Helmut, who had gathered mushrooms with her in the forests after the war. Her mother had taken care of her brother, as she had taken care of Joan, however imperfectly.

Jim, the manager, with whom she was having a little kissing affair, walked up to her from his office with a quick knock, the door open. He bumbled in immediately after knocking. Joan always felt a little shocked by his energy, how quickly he moved his large body.

"Boy, your mom sure looks beautiful today," he said. He walked up to her mother and rubbed her shoulder. Her mother stared at the wall.

Joan sat down on the bed and tapped it next to her. Jim walked over, sat down, and they kissed, her hands on his broad shoulders. He tasted like mint. Jim always chewed gum.

He looked into her eyes, his beady and blue, and said, "You sure look beautiful, too."

Joan smiled.

They had begun this flirtation the first day her mother arrived. Joan had walked into his office and needed help putting the pictures of her family and relatives in a glass frame to hang in front of her mother's room, and Jim had helped her choose the photos. He chose the one of her mother and father hiking in the Alps, the silver peaks behind them, and placed it at the top. Below, Joan pasted photos of her uncle, her sister Angelika, and one of her own family in Mexico when Jeremy and Michele were young, Joan's red hair bobbed and glinting in the sun, Jeremy with his fingers in the peace sign above Michele's head, both with Darren's dark hair and Darren looking askance at something out of the frame and smiling. When she and Jim had finished, he leaned into her, and though she didn't know him at all, she kissed the side of his head.

She felt beautiful with Jim. She also felt guilty. Well, at least she wasn't sleeping with him. He had never tried to make that happen, and they both seemed content with kissing, though he did mention once she should visit his home in Longmont after work sometime, but she had declined.

When Joan came home, her scrappy small tabby Henry was playing with a dead squirrel as big as he was on the living room floor. He was kicking his back legs against the carcass and biting its neck. Joan chased him around the house, and finally he was worn out and she was successful, since the squirrel was too heavy for him to carry. As she grabbed a plastic grocery bag, she made a note that she would need more from Safeway, even though they cost ten cents.

That evening, after visiting her anger management class and learning how to clap when you want to hit instead, breathe deeply, and analyze, she wrote a review of the restaurant for a side job she had for a local internet review site called Boulder's Best. She wrote that the combination of pesto tofu and cherry preserves with an Indian touch of saag drenched in cumin was delicious. She fed her children leftover pasta as she listened to Darren drone on and on about his body and the amazing fact that he had learned from the massage therapist that his right leg was shorter than his left. Joan thought about how much just one shot of whiskey would soothe her, but she had one year and 5 months of probation left.

Jeremy and Michele would be eighteen and sixteen, and Darren and she would be late middle-aged, approaching fifty.

Her children were unaware of her probation for the most part because Joan hid it from them out of shame. But they knew. Michele had become even more sassy, Jeremy more dismissive of Joan. Would she still be teaching in a year for Mountain View College? Should she pursue dog training instead, since she was certified for it and rarely used it? She had a degree in English and had been teaching adjunct for years, and she'd traveled to Sierra Vista, Arizona, and completed a course in dog training from the Good Dogs Academy when she and Darren were first married. In any case, she wouldn't have to sort clothing anymore. There would be an end.

She walked into the living room. It smelled like wood and dust. On the wall was a painting of horses galloping across the plains. The plush sofa invited her to sink into it, and she curled with a florid blanket across her feet. Henry jumped on her lap and fell asleep. Both of them were exhausted from a day of killing or taking care of the living.

When she rose to use the bathroom, she walked into the kitchen and found a blue feather she had failed to sweep up. It was as blue as her eyes, as blue as the skies of Colorado, as Lake Michigan, and as blue as the opal ring her mother had given her when she was in college. Joan had worn that ring every day as a teenager, but one evening when she was in college, before she met Darren, she was drinking and dancing in a club and told everyone she could read their auras if they held her ring. That night she came home without it and didn't notice until she woke up, hungover, the next day. She picked the feather up and set it on the counter. She didn't want to throw it away. She closed her eyes and stroked it. She then glanced up and saw the purple candle with an image of the Madonna in a yellow dress. She went to the kitchen drawer and pulled out a lighter. After lighting the candle, she watched the fire flicker, and she wouldn't clap because then the fire would extinguish the flame. There had to be something leftover, something that was not lost, some remnant of flight when the body disappears out of life.

Joan Is a Failure

Joan was brilliant at failing. She failed at keeping steady employment. She failed at raising her kids to be functional and happy. She was terrible at backing out of spaces in parking lots. She was abhorrent at paying her bills on time. She always forgot to keep a tampon in her purse, just in case.

She wanted to feel fulfilled and happy in life, but ever since her father's suicide, and the day she had to bring back her mother with Alzheimer's to the United States from Austria, she had a kind of nightmare experience regarding her life. When she hiked and saw sticks, she saw snakes. The dead blue jays Henry left in the kitchen as gifts for her made her cry, both the generosity of the cat and the gruesomeness of the death. At the end of the day, she would fall asleep only to wake up in the middle of the night and think of how she'd dented their old van; kissed Jim in front of the nosy resident, Sharon; ignored her dog, Filbert, and lost him for an hour in the woods; or didn't listen to a word her children said. Then she would wonder when and how she would die, and she'd be terrified while she tried to find a comfortable position in bed, her pillow between her legs, rolling sideways, then on her back, eyes closed and neck stiffening, red numbers of the clock glaring at her.

She failed to understand how the fear of her death also made it enticing to her. She often dreamed about dying: airplane crashes into the sea where she and all one hundred passengers would tumble, from the knife of a sociopath, or cancer.

When she looked at the evening sky, she always wanted to be closer to the moon, and when she looked at pictures of her father—with his freckles and red hair—she wanted to see him again to tell him off. He had always solidified her conception of herself as a failure. She wanted to fight back. To yell at him. To tell him "fuck you." She had failed to tell him how she'd really felt when he was alive.

She was even a failure at killing herself.

The first time she tried was after a Halloween party, where she dressed as a Viking princess but failed to find the horns she was supposed to wear on her head. Because she was a bit of a hoarder and stored things in her closet, the horns disappeared in a pile of puzzle pieces her son had failed to finish. He had dumped the pieces in the laundry basket of clean clothes, so they were wrapped in her old bras and sheets. So everyone asked her what she was supposed to be, clothed in a brown dress with fake fur. While her husband handed out candy and her children went to a party—Jeremy dressed as a redneck with pants made out of the American flag, Michele a black cat—Joan drank brandy. She drank a lot. She got drunk. It was not the smartest decision at the time because she was still on probation and if a day was her testing day, her probation officer would threaten her with jail. But it was too late because the brandy was swimming in her head. She thought how the house really needed to be painted and this time they should do the frame a squash color, and how life was a dead end, and at the end of it was a castle with a prince who would save her and put a crown of gold and diamonds on her head.

She would look down at the planet from a heaven she surely deserved because God forgave, and all the people who had ignored her would weep and lay flowers on her grave and the obituary would read that she was a wonderful mother and brilliant writer, and even the ex-boyfriend who left her when she was twenty because he said she was too depressing would write a poem that would be published in the New Yorker. The last line would read, "She was the rays of the full moon, the tide that carried the ships home." She would bring all that light into heaven. She would lay the light at God's feet, supplicate, and drink the holy water. Then she would tell her father, "Fuck you."

She looked at her legs she had failed to cover in stockings, the veins beginning to pop out more as she grew older. Her legs were plump, as was her whole body now that she was middle-aged. She swam regularly and walked with Filbert, but she had the big-boned build of her mother, with large breasts and hips.

She went upstairs to collect herself and saw Darren's tie hanging in the closet, the paisley purple one. She looked around for a place to tie it, then thought how hanging was a good way to go, but there was only the shower curtain rod. As she tied it to the rod, she realized she had no idea how to tie a noose. When she pulled it, the whole rod came tumbling down.

"What's going on up there?" yelled Darren from downstairs.

She swallowed, then spit into the shower. Her phlegm looked like a snail. "Nothing," she replied.

Darren came into the room and saw the tie hanging on the curtain rod. "Oh, there it is! I was looking for this tie. It's one of my favorites. My Aunt Susie gave it to me." He took the tie from her hand and turned toward the mirror and brushed his black hair.

The second time Joan tried to commit suicide was after she taught a creative writing class at Mountain View Community College where she was horrendously underpaid. It was late afternoon and the sun was slumping toward the horizon, not that she could see it because her classroom had no windows, and after class, one of her students complained that Joan's grading was unfair. He wrote a poem that had dragons and quantum physics in it.

"There is no showing here," she said, "only telling."

He scrunched his red eyebrows and said, "You just don't understand me."

Walking out to the parking lot, she concluded that she didn't understand anyone. She didn't understand any of the letters her schizophrenic father wrote, where he explained in great detail how his sex therapist and Conoco pursued him and created a new dimension of hell made out of blood. When Darren woke up at 5:00 a.m. to run ten miles in the dark, she thought he was actually as crazy as her father. When Michele told her she would never pierce her nose like Joan, she didn't understand how she could have given birth to someone so mainstream.

So she was walking to her old van with a huge dent in the fender that embarrassed her, but she was too broke to fix, and it was November, the sky steel-gray, moody clouds sitting on the horizon, and another student she'd failed passed her and scowled, his pierced lip as swollen as the clouds. She thought about how if she disappeared, everyone would be alright. Her sister Angelika could finally deal with her mother, take over caring for her, and her children liked their father better anyway. Joan rummaged through her purse and found ten Valium pills, cursing her psychiatrist who didn't let her buy two months at a time, hoping against all odds that ten would be enough. She took the handful and ate them without water, bitterness another punitive measure.

Before driving home, she stopped at King Soopers in Longmont because she wanted to make sure the family had something to eat for dinner. She parked her van with extra care. She felt elated, as if she now had made an important decision that would save her life by ending it. In the store, she bought boxes of macaroni and cheese and four bags of potato chips, the sour cream and onion kind, because that was Jeremy's favorite.

While driving, she began to feel sleepy. The road looked long before her, and time began to slow. She gripped the steering wheel and squinted, the bright sun suddenly blinding. The car in front of her was orange, and she decided orange was a stupid color for a car.

She made it home. Darren was still at work and Michele and Jeremy at school. She walked up the stairs to the bedroom, feeling dizzy, and fell asleep. When she woke up, her mouth felt pasty, and she lay in bed and looked at the painting of dancing women, their silhouettes next to the bare branches of a tree. She thought of the maple tree in front of their house in Chicago. When she was six, she used to feed the squirrels her hamster food below that tree. The seeds grew into little sunflower and millet sprouts dotting the lawn, and her father spanked her. She looked at the red light of the clock radio and closed her eyes, not registering the time. Then she looked at the clock again and it was 5:30 p.m., and she had slept over two hours.

"What the hell are you doing? The kids are hungry," Darren said as he stepped into the room. She opened her eyes and his thin body looked like those branches of the maple. His dark eyes were like the nuts on a walnut tree, dark and dry.

"You look like a tree," said Joan.

Darren sighed. "What the hell are you talking about, Joan? Anyway, what's the dinner plan?"

"I'll figure it out," she said while rising from the bed. She felt sleepy and relaxed, calm as the brooding skies of November outside. "I just need to brush my teeth." She walked to the sink, which in their 1970s home was in the bedroom, a floor plan that always annoyed her, and one she and Darren discussed as something they could change. She couldn't find her toothbrush so brushed her teeth with her finger while listening to Michele yell, "Mom!"

Michele walked into the room. "Mom, can you drive Anna and me to the mall tomorrow?" she asked. She was wearing jean shorts so short half her butt hung out of them. Her breasts, which were huge like her mother's and had developed when Michele was only eleven, leading Joan to worry about hormones in their food, were smashed in a tight cropped shirt. Her dark hair was so long Joan thought she should donate it to cancer patients, but when she'd mentioned it to Michele, Michele rolled her eyes and said, "I don't think so."

"I think I can take you," Joan said. "But no more short shorts."

Michele sighed. "You have to promise. Last time you said you would and then didn't."

Joan sighed back, resigned to experiencing another day. "Okay, I promise."

The third time she decided to attempt suicide was when she tried to purchase a handgun. Turns out you need to pass a background check, and she didn't. She had stalked a man in '92 and it sucked because she had truly loved him, and didn't love trump everything? Then she had the DUI and that assault on a police officer.

She drove to Longmont to the store Buffalo Tactical, which she had seen on Main Street once when visiting a massage therapist downtown. It was next to a bowling league she had visited occasionally with the children when they were young.

The shop was relatively empty except for a shelf of guns and rifles behind a counter with bullets and ammunition behind the glass counter. On the walls were photos of buffaloes, and a large buffalo head jutted out from the wall beside her as she walked to the counter.

The man behind the desk, his beard bushy, brown hair emerging from a baseball hat, told her how wonderful she was to be concerned about her safety. "There are some goddamn liberal punks out there ready to rape you," he said.

She glanced down at her attire. She was wearing a tight red blouse and a jean skirt that had factory-created tears in it. Wasn't that sexy? Then she remembered, appalled at her momentary ignorance, the workshop she went to once that was about how rape wasn't about sex, and she thought okay, I'm not even worth the violence to rape me.

She drove home and saw a vulture eating a dead raccoon on the road in front of their driveway. The vulture wouldn't go away, so Joan had to stop the car. She admired its trash collecting, and she thought how she, too, would feed nature with her corpse. Completely oblivious of the traffic, it was pecking at the torn carcass, bloody and smashed on the street, its black feathers scraggly, its neck so thin Joan wondered how it could even swallow so much meat. She pulled toward the bird until she almost hit its tail feathers, and it jumped out of the way. It hopped toward the curb, its pink legs the color of worms, eyes like tiny black holes.

Joan put the van in park, switched the engine off, and pulled the keys from the ignition. In the rearview mirror she watched the vulture return to his meal, the raccoon untouched by her wheels where it lay in the gutter.

In the kitchen, without the gun she'd hoped to return with, she found the cream curdling on the counter because she hadn't put it away that morning. She rummaged through the pantry and pulled out the macaroni and cheese. Once she had tried to make the homemade kind, but the kids had hated it. Anyway, she had failed to go shopping. This kind came in a box.

Jeremy and Michele loved it. They were ecstatic that they got to eat the boxed kind. Michele smiled brightly at her and told her she was a wonderful mom. Jeremy, a picky eater, dove into his bowl with relish. They slurped the noodles as if that meal were some kind of manna from heaven, a place she'd failed to arrive at.

That night Joan lay in bed with Darren, who was watching a marathon on his phone, and stared at the ceiling, then turned her head and looked at the painting of dancing women. She had failed three times to kill herself, and the women dancing were three women. She had brushed with death, but the universe wanted her to live. She was the vulture and not the raccoon. She would have to confront the waste of her life and allow it to become part of her, move through and with death into some semblance of life.

She turned her head and stared at the white ceiling and thought how homes protect you from the vast heavens, how shelter was a privilege. Darren set down his phone and sidled next to her. He kissed her cheek, and she ran her fingers through his black curls. Her eyes felt so heavy. She closed them and fell asleep to an image of dark wings.

They Did Not Fly Away

Joan had always longed for a father who was like a lion, regal and powerful, and then she longed for a husband who would be like this, but when she was a freshman in college, she met Darren, who was no Leo. A Virgo, he was no lion but a skinny runner who knew how to build houses, and Joan wanted a home.

She and Darren hiked together while she studied English, and he studied biology. He worked in construction to pay for his studies, which he eventually quit, content to work and run. She and Darren went to concerts together and in the summer took road trips in his beat-up green Beetle. They withstood sandstorms in Arizona, camped on Lake Superior's shore, and drove up to Montreal and met a man who let them stay in his apartment, where they awoke in the night to cockroaches crawling on their legs. Darren built frames, constructed cabinets, built decks, and on his weeks off ran 25-mile routes in the mountains in one day, passing by people who had taken two days to hike those distances for backcountry camping.

They married when Joan was a junior, much to her parents' dismay, who thought Joan should have married a man with more money and education. At the wedding, a small outdoor affair at the foot of the mountains, Joan got so drunk that by the end of the evening she saw two faces when she looked at Darren. This drunken blur of perception would continue throughout their marriage: he was two things to Joan—a grounding force and a man who would always run away, a homebuilder who never tried to nail her down.

She liked how he cooked her rattlesnake sausage for dinner and wandered the woods when he wasn't busy working construction. Once when he killed a goose for Christmas dinner, he covered it in hot chile sauce and kissed her and told her she was the best Christmas present he'd ever had. That was when their two children were young. When he wasn't leaving her alone with the kids, he was kind.

Yet marriage and living in the suburbs changed him. He became more and more controlling, not of her but everything else, like his body. He also developed a passion for reading blogs about sports on his phone and blared soccer, football, or bike racing on their television all evening.

As a teenager, she'd wanted a father like Aslan from *The Chronicles of Narnia*. Like Lucy, Joan would bury her head in his mane and become a lioness. But her father was more like a vulture, pecking at the roadkill of his psychotic mind, his thoughts all too often brutalized by bouts of paranoid schizophrenia. Darren had become more like a geometry equation, all lines and graphs and angles as he calculated everything, including every bite of food he ate so he could be skeletal for his long-distance runs and triathlons. Often Joan wanted to be seen or listened to but felt invisible. The marriage remained convenient, and sometimes fulfilling. While he chiseled his life and body to a form with little room for her, she took care of her demented mother and the children, wrote occasional food reviews, and taught English.

Sometimes they walked together on the plains, and he built bridges over the ditches for her. When she was pregnant, he would spoon her and cup his hands over her belly, tell her she was beautiful. When her pregnancy heightened her sense of smell and she couldn't even stand garbage in the house, he would buy her lilies and lavender air freshener.

But because their children were older, and Joan was kissing Jim and plagued with guilt, Joan decided they should work on their relationship and signed them up for a Gotman marriage workshop because it was called *The Art and Science of Love*, and Darren always respected science, and she art. She would change. She would become committed.

She texted her friend Alyssa, *I think it might help.*

Joan was sitting on the couch in the living room with Henry on her lap and outside it was snowing lightly.

That's bullshit, Joan. Just visit me with the money instead.

Joan thought about it. She would love to visit Alyssa, but traveling was so difficult logistically with her DUI, and anyway all she had was a weekend because of her teaching schedule.

I've gotta connect with Darren, she wrote. *But I do miss you.*

Well, hope it's worth it, sweetie. Gotta go. Seth just broke a vase.

They sent each other heart emojis and Joan leaned back on the couch and sighed. She missed Alyssa, who had been one of her sister Angelika's friends and whom she'd known since they were children. Alyssa had moved to Boulder for college when Joan was married to Darren and they both got pregnant with their first children at the same time. Angelika actually lost contact with her for the most part and Alyssa became more Joan's friend. She was seven years younger than her and had astounding fertility. Alyssa had five children. She married young like Joan, and they both now had teenagers, but Alyssa kept having children and Joan stopped at two.

The week before the workshop, Joan drove to Into the Light and smoked a cigarette in the parking lot while trying to think what to say. She would make it about her and not him, tell him that she was cheating on her husband and felt guilty. Before her lay a huge parking lot practically empty of cars. It made her sad that so many people didn't visit the residents.

She walked up the hallway and into the Alzheimer's unit. Jim was serving nosy Sharon bacon. She pulled him into the medicine room and she told him that she needed to work on her marriage, and as she leaned against the locked safe of medicine, she knocked it over.

"It's just over. I'm sorry." Joan looked into his blue eyes, then wept.

Jim shrugged and wiped his nose. He asked, "Are you sure?"

She assured him she was. "I have to get my life together," she said as she put her hands in his pocket, knowing he pocketed Valium. She fingered the pills and closed her fist around them, then rubbed as if she were caressing and comforting him. "I'm sick of lying."

"Boy, Darren is a lucky man," he said while shaking his head. He was big and strong, and although bald and missing the golden mane she dreamed of, and his nose was tiny and his eyes small, he was a bit of a lion in stature.

She cupped his cheek and said, "You knew I was married."

"But we were getting together," he said. "Geez, I really love your mom."

Joan thought how the whole scenario had started for that reason. He loved her mom. Darren had nothing to do with her life around her mom. She thought of how Jim dressed as Santa Claus and put her children on his lap, and she felt like gagging. She should have asked Darren to play Santa. She should have asked. She had been so wrong. "I'm sorry," she said.

That night she cried in her bedroom as Darren watched a rerun of last year's World Cup.

On a cold January day, Joan and Darren drove together in silence. The drive on the tollway was socked in fog and snarled in traffic. They arrived at the hotel, a white building with green trim.

The conference room in the hotel was cold, and Joan opened her suitcase at the check-in counter and pulled on her black wool cardigan. She absolutely dreaded spending two full days with Darren. It was a sprawling suburb, and the view from the hotel room was of a gigantic golf course covered in snow and a pond full of geese walking on the ice.

Tables were set up to fit each couple, and she and Darren arrived late, so they ended up in the front row. A plastic cup filled with Snickers and Butterfingers sat in the center of the table next to a gigantic box with a booklet and decks of cards called "Open-ended Questions," "Rituals of Connection," and "Salsa," the latter full of ideas to improve a couple's sex life. While Darren approached fucking the same way he did any other physical exertion (determined to build muscle), Joan couldn't remember the last time, if ever, they had made love.

The facilitator, Kim, was a brunette with perfectly styled shoulder-length hair and a bright red blouse. The other participants were seated and staring intently at the screen, which displayed a photo of Kim and her husband sitting on an ATV with the mountains behind them. One man wore a suit and sat in the front row with his wife, who sported a blue dress and golden hoop earrings. The other participants were more casual in their attire, wearing jeans or spandex. Joan felt like how she always felt in her neighborhood, for example around Kate, out of kilter with the kings and queens of suburbia, wearing thrift-store clothes like the striped dress and leggings she was wearing now.

Throughout the day, they watched videos and listened to lectures. In one video, a mother played with her baby who gurgled and laughed on a highchair, pointing at objects in the kitchen. The mother responded to the baby with eye contact and cooing. Then she turned cold and didn't respond to the baby's constant laughter and splayed hands, and the baby began to fuss and cry, squirming in her seat, screeching to get the mother's attention. The presentation was supposed to teach them how important it is to communicate and engage, how harmful stonewalling was. All it did was make Joan cry for the poor baby in the experiment. It was like when she'd read about kittens brought up isolated in a box. They became so psychically damaged they couldn't function. It was supposed to prove that intimacy and contact was important to development. Duh. Joan decided that she hated science. She turned to Darren. He was watching the screen, his jaw tight, his eyes squinting, his curly hair brushing his cheek. She wondered what he was thinking.

Joan ate the entire bowl of candy and felt nauseous while they were discussing deep breathing and time-outs. Kim encouraged the participants to breathe deeply with her. Raising her hands, palms up in front of her, she told them to inhale and count to ten, then counted down for the exhale. The participants all breathed loudly, and Joan felt like she was suffocating because she really needed less than ten long seconds to inhale and exhale.

That evening, Darren and she bought a bottle of cognac and drank half of it after eating dinner at a cheap Mexican restaurant where Joan ate the worst enchilada she'd ever had, and Darren ate a side of salad with no dressing. She thought about what she would say if she wrote a review. She would definitely mention that the enchilada sauce was too thick, as if they had used a large quantity of corn starch. Also, the chicken was rubbery, like airplane food. It certainly had enough salt.

When they returned to the hotel, Darren put his arm around her waist and ushered her through the door, and she thought of the cognac. Joan rarely cheated on probation, but she had filled out a form lying, saying she would be out of town for a week, so she had three days after drinking to clear the alcohol out of her system so that if she got tested, it would come out negative. Joan also had managed to get a note from her psychiatrist that benzos were allowed, since her psychiatrist prescribed Valium for panic attacks. Joan rarely suffered from them, but when she did nothing else helped—not baths, dunking her head in cold water, or deep breathing. She tried to make the prescription last so that her psychiatrist didn't flag her for abusing it. Now she had some from Jim's pocket, though, which made her happy.

They entered the room, green carpet like at the nursing home, a white bed with a stained wooden bed frame, and Joan sat down on a black chair and opened the cognac. The taste of cognac was comforting, and the Valium she pilfered from Jim made her happy. She thought about the babies she'd had and loved. She reminded herself that many kittens still are raised by their mother. She loved the mellow taste of cognac in the winter, how it warmed her blood.

They built a fire and had sex. They covered her breasts in honey, an idea they got from the "Salsa" cards in the workshop. The honey felt cold, and when Darren reached to set it on the bedside table, it dribbled on the bed, and Joan got honey on her shoulder and in her hair. Darren peered at her large, saggy tits and crooned, "Joan, you're beautiful." He stroked her red hair and the sticky honey pulled at strands and hurt. She gazed at him as he returned to face her after licking her nipples. His face looked doubled, and Joan realized how drunk she was, and she cried again.

"What's wrong?" he asked. His dark curls draped over his chiseled cheeks.

"Nothing," she replied. "I'm just tired."

His black hair drank the firelight, the room was warm, and Joan came hard, and after taking another Valium, she slept like a baby (a cliché that never made sense to her, as her babies had never slept).

On the second day, after Darren woke up at five in the morning to do a ten-mile run, they had to process conflict. They left the main conference room to work in pairs wherever they wanted to in the hotel with a list of directions. They found a spot on a leather couch. In front of them was a fireplace, but there was no fire. Joan shivered. While the overhead florescent lights flickered, Joan tried to do it right, and when she told him she felt ignored when he read newspapers and watched sports instead of emotionally supporting her, Joan said, "I feel lonely, abandoned."

Darren frowned. He rubbed his freshly shaven chin. "I do so much for this family. I work my ass off all day and my body is a wreck because of it, and all you do is insult me!"

"Right, all I do! And of course, this has to be about you!" She pulled at a strand of hair, put it into her mouth, and chewed. "Forget the dinners, the laundry, the constant fucking caretaking. Forget taking care of your fucking babies while you read blogs and run marathons. Forget getting no support from you with my mother." She tried to breathe deeply. She gave him the time-out signal, her outstretched hand.

Darren stared at her with his dark eyes. "I have been working my ass off supporting the family. You make a penny for every one hundred dollars I make. You are such a bitch."

Joan stood up and scrunched her hands into fists. "Well, you're an asshole!" she yelled.

Kim was standing in the corner near the stairway of the hotel and observing the participants. She rushed over and gently asked, "Can I help you two?"

Joan reviewed all the rules that they had just broken—defensiveness, contempt, name-calling. "No," she said. "We're doing great."

Darren clenched his jaw and turned his head, staring at the empty fireplace.

With tight lips, Kim smiled. "Just please refrain from yelling," she said before walking to the other leader.

Joan watched as they both whispered in their direction, shaking their heads. She felt ashamed and said, "Darren, let's just try to get along."

"We usually do," he said. "This workshop is bullshit."

Joan and Darren left the workshop early, before the closing lecture.

On the ride home, they listened to grunge music. Soundgarden sang about a black hole sun washing away the rain, and Joan wondered how the sun could wash away the rain when it needed rain to wash. Can you wash with light? Then she realized that no, it had to be a black hole.

Joan drove because she hated Darren's driving, which consisted of making a race out of everything, constantly switching lanes and passing every car. She would criticize him, and he would yell at her and say, "Then you do the goddamn driving." She did.

Joan thought of visiting Seattle and the bands she saw in warehouses near Lake Union on a trip with friends while Darren was in a triathlon in Miami. One band was led by a woman drummer with long blond hair, the drum set on the center of the stage, the rhythm like running antelope where lions roamed on the savannah and fed their young. She thought about how disappointed she'd been when the song, "My Love is Alive" by Gary Wright wasn't "My Love is a Lion," a mondegreen that had stayed with her for years, which Joan had belted out in the car as a teenager. But maybe love being alive is enough. It doesn't have to be a lion. Joan's love was always alive; of that she didn't doubt. Darren was a good man. He probably didn't cheat on her as she did on him, he put food on the table, and his almond eyes sometimes made her dizzy. When everything in her life became lost, he was always there in their home—doubled as nails are, sturdy and wounding.

The sun was setting and the plains were swathes of yellow grass punctuated by snow. Geese congregated near a small man-made pond, some on the ice with patches of snow, some on the yellow plains. Joan turned up the heat in the car and released the remnants of cold in her body. Maybe her love was a goose. Back in Chicago—where the winters were long and bitter—the geese always migrated south once autumn fell away and the first snows came. But here in Colorado they seemed content to peck at the dead grass. They did not fly away.

In the Big, Hungry Skies

Joan wanted to reupholster her life. She wanted to get rid of the greens and blues and replace those colors with bright red, patterned with purple pansies and white daisies. She also wanted to burn all her journals and rid herself of her wardrobe, her old dusty manuscripts, her house, and her past. She wanted her mother not to have such a terminal disease and her family to listen to her more. Joan wanted to start over, but she felt that somehow her world needed her in the way an engine needs oil, she the invisible element tucked in a car to help it run.

Yet oil needs to be changed every three months, and Joan didn't get replenished. After pondering this dilemma, she decided to get a pedicure.

Her father had never loved her, but he had loved her feet. Small, with high arches and delicate toes, her feet were beautiful. Joan also respected her feet for their tenacious ability to be grounded in those moments she wasn't tripping, unlike her mind—a tangled bundle of live wires zapping tongues of fire into the sky.

On a sunny winter day, she and Michele drove to the salon, where they sat and drank diet Coke, ate M&Ms, and had their feet bathed in warm water, covered in oil, and massaged. When the kind Tibetan woman cradled Joan's feet in her hands as she trimmed, filed, and painted Joan's toes bright red, Joan looked at her beautiful feet and cried. The woman looked up at her. "Are you alright?"

"I'm just having a long day," said Joan. She looked at her big toe and it looked like a colorful worm.

Michele touched her arm. "I'm sorry, Mom." She handed her the entire bowl of M&Ms. Joan took it and cradled it in her lap. She decided to eat all the red ones first.

When she ate the last one, she choked and coughed, and the whole room of the polished and trendy women stared at her. A kind small woman with green eye shadow gave her a glass of water, but then with all the crying and snot, it didn't help. Finally, she collected herself and commented on the print on the wall of a black cat next to a smiling Asian woman. The cat had hungry eyes.

"What a great picture," she slobbered. Then she cried again. Cats were so loyal, even though they weren't loyal. Joan loved cats.

Michele frowned and leaned toward her, whispering, "Mom, try to get it together."

Joan took deep breaths and mumbled, "Sorry."

The pedicure just hadn't been enough, though Joan admired her feet every day afterward, the way the red popped out and claimed the world.

The next week, when the red polish was already beginning to chip, she was driving home from Costco, her car stuffed with energy bars, coffee, juice, salmon, cheese, and every kind of food imaginable that somehow her teenage children consumed in great quantities, when she saw the exit that would take her on the highway toward I25 going North. She took the exit, her mind buzzing with visions of wind, grass, orange rock, buffalo, and cowboys. She was heading to Wyoming.

In the car, feeling elated, she contemplated her destination. She'd been to Yellowstone with all its geysers and buffalo and tourists; she'd seen a rodeo in Cheyenne; but she had never been to Thermopolis, and Joan loved hot springs. In fact, the only things she liked about cold weather were hot tubs, blankets, and tea. It was a cold, cold world they lived in, with all its guns and dying planet and morons for presidents—cold enough so that every chance she had, she sought out heat.

The drive was relatively uneventful, as was any drive through the nothingness of Wyoming. Joan chewed an entire package of peppermint gum, sang to the radio, belting the lyrics to Alice Merton's "No Roots," stopping occasionally at rest stops to snack on her Costco provisions of Cheez-its and peanut butter-filled pretzels, and gazed at the cattle and rolling yellow landscape, sprinkled with patches of snow. She wondered what her husband would make the kids for dinner, since the dinner plan of salmon and spinach was slowly rotting in the back of the car and beginning to smell like an Alaskan fishing boat.

Once she arrived in the town, she checked into the Days Inn, a hotel filled with more dead animals than a slaughterhouse, which, considering she was in Wyoming, was saying a lot. Covering the walls were the heads of buffalo, deer, mountain lions, and antelope. On the blue carpet an entire mountain lion stared at her with yellow marbles eyes. Joan felt like they were following her, and she began to worry, but she couldn't think why, so instead she went into her room, watched television, and slept after sending a quick text to Darren: *Just getting some space*, then turned off her phone. She dreamed about leading a lame horse as it limped down a steep, rocky hill.

The next day she ate the make-it-yourself waffle covered in syrup and drank the weak coffee into which she dumped a packet of hot chocolate powder. Then she went to the Wyoming Dinosaur Center.

In the past, she had brought Jeremy to the Natural History Museum in Denver numerous times to gaze at the dinosaur skeletons. Like all toddler boys, he especially loved the Tyrannosaurus Rex with its giant, sharp teeth, since he was in that phase that many young boys experience where they want to kill every ant, worm, friend, and mother. As then, she felt mostly awe. She gazed at the 27-foot placoderms, huge fish suspended from the ceiling, and Demetrodon, which had a gigantic sail along its back. The sign said they had no idea why it had a sail: swimming, camouflage, to attract a mate? She remembered how frustrated Jeremy had been that T-Rex had such tiny arms and nobody could tell him why. Once he asked her and told her she was the mom so she should know, and she said no one knew, so he hit her shins with his tiny fists and told her she was stupid. She wondered whether he won the ultimate Frisbee game the day before. She took a deep breath and took in all the ribs, femurs, and mysterious sails. She liked looking at bones. Joan thought of her bones, which made her think of her beautiful feet, which made her happy.

Her phone buzzed and she looked at it. Darren had written, *Where the hell is the can opener?* She answered, *Top right drawer, next to the sink.*

Joan practically had the rinky-dink museum to herself. There was a family with a young boy and a baby in the stroller wrapped in a flannel blanket, and an older woman wearing turquoise earrings in the shape of feathers. One old man with a badge that read "Volunteer" guarded the place. He was wearing brown pants and a green T-shirt with a slogan: "Jesus and the Dinosaurs," with Jesus in a white robe lifting his hands and surrounded in light, circled by four dinosaurs.

When she saw the bones of the Archaeoptergidae embraced by the sunset-colored stone, she got herself in a bit of trouble. The fossil had a second toe, which provided evidence that it was almost avian, and Joan knew it right away: She was meant to fly. It was set in orange stone, and the bones reminded Joan of herself, lovingly placed in all its dying. She was staring at its claw-like feet and thinking of flight, of dinosaurs cruising the skies, of a world with no people, just giant creatures and rocks and air and bone and before she knew it, she climbed over the rope and grabbed the fossil, then turned and ran toward the exit.

The overweight, old volunteer walked toward her and yelled, "Hey, stop!" He shuffled behind her as Joan ran. She tripped and glanced behind her. He was yelling, "You will go to court for this!" Joan ran but his lumbering body began gaining ground, and anyway, her left ankle hurt. She tripped, but her sturdy feet found the ground again, and she made it to her car. She unlocked it and glanced behind her, where the man was still yelling, "Thief! Filth!" She didn't even fumble with her keys. She was used to holding her ignition key between her two fingers to gouge out the eyes of someone who might sexually assault her. It took her very little time to drive away. She hoped he hadn't read her license plate number. She decided he wasn't bright enough to think that fast let alone memorize a combo of letters and numerals. Then she felt bad about thinking so little about a complete stranger and she hoped he wouldn't get into too much trouble because of her.

Later, while soaking in the hot springs after staring at the Big Horn River from the Swinging Bridge, its water meandering like her thoughts, she thought about her dead father, the advantages and disadvantages of indica versus sativa, and what color her aging dog Filbert's aura was (she figured green; he was very social). She wondered how Michele did on her math test, and whether Jeremy ever asked his crush out. She contemplated where she would put her fossil if she returned home. She decided next to her bed, where she had a collection of crystals Michele had given her.

The next day she got in her car after calling to find out if it was a testing day, which it wasn't. The salmon from Costco was rotting, and because she was feeling a little guilty, she decided she would just drive home with the smell to punish herself for abandoning her family, who was probably faltering, starving, desperate without her. Michele probably couldn't find the ketchup and needed money—she always needed money—and Jeremy needed Band-Aids and couldn't find socks, and Darren was probably watching porn and weeping since all the women would make him think of Joan. The dog would be dehydrated since only Joan filled his water bowl, and the plants, too, would be thirsty, wilting, and yellow-leaved. She also felt a little guilty for stealing the dinosaur fossil. Kind of. She had placed it in the glove compartment and there it lay, leading her to a flight home.

As she breathed in the rotting stench, she gazed at the landscape. The day was sunny, and the Wyoming sky large and blue. She thought about California and its Pacific, its skies over the ocean bigger than any creature that ever existed on this Earth. As she drove, a hawk dived over her car and flew toward an orange butte. It looked like it had a purpose, like it was hunting for something in the dry landscape—in the big, hungry skies.

When she returned home, it was dark, and she peeked into the dining room window. Jeremy was eating a hot dog with no bun and scrolling on his phone, and Michele was scowling at Darren, who was laughing and picking his teeth. Filbert was lying in the corner, chewing on a bone.

She thought again about California. They were due for a visit to Alyssa and family. She needed to call Alyssa and tell her about the dinosaur fossil. She had failed to become a wrangler of anything but bones in Wyoming, but maybe in California she would surf, glide on the giant waves, befriend the dolphins and whales and learn their language. Her beautiful feet would hold her steady on the board, and she would fly.

Grateful

It was a Sunday in April, and Joan had ten more months of probation. Darren and she were planting seeds in their garden, sweating and plunging their fingers into the tilled soil to plant beans.

Every year they planted a garden, and every year they argued about who would do the weeding. They both refused, and so the weeds would quickly drown all their efforts, and Joan would try to find the lettuce and give up.

She tried to read the notes of how deep to plant the seeds and peered at the packets of beans and kale, but she was getting far-sighted, so she decided the length of her finger to her knuckle should be good for any seed. And anyway, were seeds that picky? They certainly weren't if they were related to sperm, which impregnated her immediately if she miscalculated one damn day of her ovulation. She'd just popped two babies out of her right after another as soon as she got off the pill, after she and Darren had already been together for seven years. She hadn't even had her period once after Jeremy was born, and wham, then she was pregnant with Michele. She planted the beans around the corner of the garden bed and then stopped to stare at a beetle, its black back like charred wood.

While pruning a raspberry bush, Joan thought briefly about her children. She had no idea where they were.

The phenomena in Boulder of helicopter parenting seemed to have passed her by, though she was in respectful awe of all the mothers out there who were so attentive. Jeremy was probably playing ultimate Frisbee or smoking a vape pipe at the neighborhood park, or maybe he was in his room playing League of Legends. Michele was probably painting her toenails black or taking selfies to send to her friends.

Joan was thirsty, and her back ached.

She stood up and stretched, thinking of her mother's garden in the Midwest, with ripe tomatoes, current bushes for jam, and spinach they ate every night in the summer.

Entering the home to drink a glass of water, she detected an ashen, chemical smell, the odor of rayon or some other industrial product burning, a smokiness not of campfires or burning leaves but of an industry circling a city and hiding its toxic magic in ovens, and Joan's heart stuck in her throat as she coughed and climbed the stairs to a thin gray cloud and wondered again where her children were.

The house was on fire.

"Michele, Jeremy!" she yelled as she ran up the stairs. The air was the color of ash, and the door to the bathroom was closed, so she opened it to see a blue towel crumpled on the floor that she'd forgotten to put in the laundry after swimming. A tube of toothpaste lay leaking on the sink, and a spider crawled across the toilet seat. Joan then looked into Michele's room, with her bed scrunched up and unmade, nail polish stacked neatly in a row on her shelf next to seashells she'd found in Mexico and California. A conch shell with its pink mouth open to the gray air. A penny on the floor. Joan bolted out the door and rushed to the studio. Michele was sitting at her desk poring over a Seventeen magazine.

"Get out!" yelled Joan.

"God, Mom," Michele said, "don't yell at me!" She looked up at Joan, her long black strands dangling over her cheeks, then her eyes opening with realization as she looked at Joan's expression, full of fear.

Joan felt something well in her gut and a fly was buzzing, twirling loudly around the window. "There's a fire, get out!"

Michele ran down the stairs and out the front door, and Joan rushed out of the studio down the hallway and looked toward Jeremy's room, the door closed. She yelled, but there was no reply. The smoke was getting thicker, and she couldn't see more than two feet in front of her now, so she raced downstairs to get Darren.

Joan was shaking. The sun had that mellow sharpness of a Colorado April, and she thought briefly how she wanted a cigarette.

She went into the backyard. Their dog, Filbert, was lying on the grass next to the garden beds. "Darren, the house is on fire!"

Kneeling on the dirt pathway between garden beds, Darren was planting squash seeds, his thin body angular in the bright sun, catching light like tree twigs, his shadow a dark stain on the green grass. Filbert raised his head and panted. "What tires?" he asked without looking up. "I put them in your car already."

Joan then ran to him and yelled because ever since Darren turned forty-seven, he was hard of hearing. "Fire!" she screamed, "the house is on fire!" She grabbed his arm, his flesh a salty river and a cloud cut off the sun. Filbert came to her and sniffed her leg.

Darren squinted, sweat streaking his face and a smudge of dirt on his cheek, and then they both ran to the front of the house. They looked for Jeremy's car, a junky old Toyota Corolla with a sticker on it that said, Live to Run. It was parked right in front of the house, meaning that Jeremy was probably home, so they ran inside through the front door. They looked up the stairs that led to the second floor when you walk in. Joan cursed herself for assuming Jeremy wasn't home, not even bothering to open his door, which had scared her with its thick smoke streaming out of it and the heat, and she had not been thinking, and now Darren was convinced Jeremy was in his room and what if he was right? The muscles in her gut contracted and her hands began to shake.

"Jeremy!" yelled Darren. He turned and went to the spigot in the front, walked to the door again, then returned.

Darren hooked up the hose. By now all they saw through the front door was a sheet of black. He tried to walk through it to get to Jeremy's door, dragging the hose behind him. "I can't see anything!" he said.

He dropped the hose and turned to go into the garage and got a sledgehammer. Joan watched him swing it as he ran into the house and disappeared into what now looked like a solid black wall of something thicker than smoke.

While Joan called 911, Michele was crying and her tall body shook, her checkered pajama pants long and touching the green lawn next to the old willow tree they had trimmed to keep it from falling on their roof, and when Joan got off the phone, they stared at the smoke and heard a crashing sound and yells. "It's just the sledgehammer," she told Michele, who was standing next to her and crying, and Joan hoped that was all the sound was, and not the ceiling falling on her son or husband.

Neighbors began to mill about, and one of them, a woman whom Joan only knew from watching her work endlessly on her flawless landscaping, pruning the roses and weeding the bindweed off her petunias, asked whether they had tried to call Jeremy. Kate was also there and wearing a purple tennis dress and holding a racket. She approached Joan and put her hand on Joan's shoulder. "Have you called Jeremy? Are you sure he's in there?"

Darren was covered in soot and racing out of the house to get a ladder. He set it against the house and climbed to Jeremy's window, broke the glass, and turned his sooty face to her as she watched him. "I can't see!" he yelled. The water coming out of the hose fell onto the side of the house, its thin dribble looking so inadequate, so desperate.

Joan was calling Jeremy on her phone, but she couldn't hear anything. Sirens punctuated the sky and her neighbors hovered around her talking. The old man Devon from next door who owned chickens despite the neighborhood bear, stood with his arms akimbo and the psychologist Summer was pressing her palms together as if in prayer. Then Jeremy picked up the phone.

"Yeah," he said instead of hello.

"Oh, Jesus," she said, "you're okay." A trickle of sweat dripped into her eyes. She coughed. It felt like something was stuck in her throat and she kept coughing.

"You alright?" he said. "I got a haircut today. What's up? You sound upset."

"Where are you?" Joan's voice was tight and she coughed again.

"I'm at Eli's." Eli was a neighbor.

A spasm descended into her belly. "Jeremy, the house is on fire. Come home."

"Shit, I heard the sirens. I'll be right there."

Joan looked up at Darren. He turned toward her and looked down, sledgehammer raised, broken window. His eyes were hollow, and his jeans were covered in dirt.

"He's okay!" she yelled.

Darren descended from the ladder and turned toward them, frozen, his face black and hair singed, curling white at the edges. The expression on his face was a mixture of relief and shock. It was ghost-like and reminded Joan of a corpse, ashen and frozen, the eyes like deep pockets full of copper grief and fear. His eyes fell on her while flames licked at him out the window, Joan sweating, waving her arms at him, telling him to get down, the silver ladder rickety and leaning, Darren like a ghost.

Sirens blared, fire trucks came, and the firemen broke more windows for the hoses. An ambulance arrived and paramedics walked quickly across the front lawn, the sky fleeced of clouds but for the dark tendril of smoke, her stomach crunching as if giving birth but really she just needed to shit, the driveway with cracks and rising fissures, and her daughter surrounded by the firemen in their armor. When she tried to stop them to ask them what to do, they pushed her aside. They grabbed Darren's arms and led him into the ambulance, and she followed them, tripped on a buckled piece of the sidewalk, and rummaged in her pocket for a cigarette that wasn't there. The dark-haired paramedic pulled at Darren's arm and Kate tapped her shoulder, and Joan turned her head toward her but walked away, following Darren. All she could do was enter the ambulance with him. The firemen yelled at each other outside, but Joan couldn't make out what they were saying. The neighbors milled about, talking to each other, staring at the house with its broken eyes and fire and soot and ash, and Jeremy and Michele walked with her to the ambulance and stood outside, peering in.

Joan sat next to Darren where he lay with his dirty work jeans and his green tie-dyed T-shirt that the children always teased him about because he was such a hippy in some ways. That was the part of Darren Joan liked, the scrappy man who liked the woods and camping, who could build a fire and contain it and even now, with the oxygen mask over his face and the paramedic telling her the obvious, that he suffered smoke inhalation, and she could see how Darren was going to rescue them somehow and at the same time he would not provide the living in the shelter, but he would build the shelter, not the living in it, the cooking and cleaning and parenting because the shelter had always been about her, the domesticity of the anima that she carried for him, the sheering and feeding of what was wild that she resented and embraced at the same time. Joan grabbed his sweaty hand in the box of metal and machine, and he kept trying to take the mask off to speak to her but the paramedic, a small man with black hair and glasses, kept putting the mask back on Darren's face and saying he just needed to breathe.

Jeremy returned and his back was hunched as he looked into the ambulance, his tall body leaning toward the unforgiving earth, hair dark as storm clouds. "Sorry you thought I was home, Mom."

The paramedic turned to her and said, "We're going to take your husband to the hospital, just to be safe."

"I'm fine," said Darren, pulling the oxygen mask off his face again.

Joan said, "He's fine," feeling guilty because a part of her was just worried about the hospital bill they would have to pay. The paramedic said, "He inhaled a lot of smoke. It's the safe thing to do."

Joan hated hospitals, the blinking machines. The nurses in scrubs. "But he's breathing oxygen now."

The man sighed and rubbed his chin. "People can stop breathing when they've inhaled too much smoke. It's up to you. I'm just advising you."

Joan looked into Darren's eyes while he shrugged and said, "Alright," then pulled his hand away from her and pushed the mask back over his mouth.

Joan's car was in the driveway and she would meet them in the hospital. But first she wanted to go into the house, now wet and black. Her neighbor Stephanie touched her arm. She had worked a job as a real estate agent and now was retired and painted landscapes with no people in them, just trees and fields. Stephanie had been a drug addict as a teen and collected so many chips at NA but threw them all away because when she moved for the last time, she'd been sober for ten years. She hugged Joan and told her that they could stay at her house. Kate walked to her, tennis racket still in hand, and asked what she could do. Everyone was offering them shelter, neighbors who normally engaged in persiflage now full of wonder and horror, but Joan couldn't think that far ahead but she said yes, okay, thank you, and for a moment she saw them sleeping on clean sheets, but then she looked at a twig on the ground and startled because she thought it was a snake.

"We have a room upstairs for you," Kate said.

Joan nodded and looked at the house.

She wondered when she could go inside to get her dinosaur fossil, which she kept with crystals in her bedside cabinet. It was good luck and helped her sleep, she was sure. The smoke had cleared but the windows were shattered, slivers of glass glinting on the lawn, openings black with jagged spikes like teeth. Joan needed to see what had happened. The fire was out and she smelled smoke, bitter and acrid, firemen wearing masks and stringing orange tape to block entry. She walked across the lawn still strewn with last year's willow leaves, and a fireman in his yellow suit and black mask pulled up to his forehead stopped her.

"You can't go in there," he said, lightly touching her arm.

Joan pushed him aside and kept walking toward the front door.

The man grabbed her arm again, this time not gently, and said, "Ma'am, it's dangerous," and as she tore the orange tape blocking her from the house, she turned to kick him, and he grabbed both her arms and yelled in her face, "I know this is hard for ya'll, but you just can't go in! Be patient."

Joan crumpled on the ground and a wet willow branch poked her. She began weeping. She wanted to call her mother, but her mother was nonverbal with Alzheimer's, and Joan thought how thin the skin felt on her mother's hand, how even still she recognized Joan. She felt like she was going to choke, and when she closed her eyes all she could see was black. What if Jeremy had been in his room and she hadn't tried to save him? Her stomach twisted, the intestines gnarled branches of her life that she never trimmed enough to clear the way of her thinking, and Michele was sobbing on the sidewalk. The fireman crouched down to sit next to Joan on the wet grass. "You will sort this out. We'll get you in contact with people who will help. Your insurance company has already be notified. Just be thankful ya'll are okay."

Joan lifted her head and looked at him. Unshaven. Blond hair. He held her arm. She thought how much she wanted a cigarette. She thought about the whiskey in the kitchen. In the copse of trees next to her house she thought she saw a silver streak run toward the back fence. Her cat. Henry. She needed to find Henry. She tried to run to the backyard but they had taped the entry through the gate, too, and two firemen guarded the gate.

One of them walked to her and asked whether she was going to the hospital with her husband and she glanced behind her at the empty spot where the ambulance had been and said yes. She combed her hand through her hair and found her keys in the pocket with her other. On the way to the hospital, the kids still staying in front of the house, her hands shook. She focused as hard as she could on the road, but she felt as if she'd forgotten how to drive. She was like a child learning how to dive through waves to not get pummeled by them, and the waves were panic building into her bones.

In the hospital, a therapy dog came into the ER. Where was Filbert? Joan imagined he was still in the backyard and she needed to feed him and would they have to buy new pet food? And what about her dinosaur fossil? Would it smell like smoke now? The stone was limestone and is limestone porous? Would it absorb this awful smell of smoke that wafted off Darren's body now?

Joan pet the dog's brindled back while Darren breathed oxygen, and the numbers blinked and blinked. It was a Pitbull mix, and its eyes were dark and reassuring. Joan decided then and there that they would get another dog, which made her think of Henry again and wonder where he was. He so often liked to doze in Jeremy's room, but the room had been closed so he'd probably been outside during the fire. Joan felt a well of panic rise from her heart to her eyes.

When they released Darren, reeking of smoke and hair curled and frizzled with gray tips like a burning cigarette, she drove with him back to the house. The firemen were still congregating, and most of the neighbors had returned home for dinner.

This time they let them in, and Joan walked into the kitchen. A huge puddle lay on the floor, and all the white walls had turned an orange-brown color. She climbed the stairs and looked down the hallway. The painting of her father with the background of sunflowers was covered in soot. Jeremy's room was blocked off with a cross of orange tape. The fireman followed her and told her that she couldn't take anything and that all the clothes would need to be cleaned. There was water everywhere. All the walls were like a smoggy sunset and when Darren asked the man what they could take, the man said they couldn't take anything.

"You need to get replacements for your meds," he said. "All the medication is ruined."

They walked back down the stairs and Joan retrieved a bottle of whiskey, the only thing she carried out of the house. She placed it in the back of the car, kissed Darren, and went to the pharmacy. She told the Asian woman at the counter, with the most perfectly smooth skin of anyone Joan had ever met, about the fire. The woman looked at her with pity.

For weeks afterward she would smell smoke while walking the dog, shopping for supplies, poring over insurance documents. They had to throw their clothes away in the hotel with its perfect white sheets, where she spent two weeks making phone calls and posting requests on Next Door for a rental while they build. Joan took care of finding shelter and caring for the family while Darren dealt with insurance and rebuilding. Joan took Filbert with her everywhere because she couldn't leave him alone in the hotel, and the moody skies of April rained on them when they walked on the trail near the hotel. It was on the southeast side of Boulder, with trails more crowded than what she was used to. She'd wear her woolen blue coat in the rain and the leggings and T-shirt a friend gave her, and she and Filbert would dodge the people and other dogs, and sometimes Joan just wanted to be alone and rest but there was so much to do.

As the weeks progressed, Darren coughed up black soot for days, the walls and floors of their house were torn down, and they bought underwear and soap and learned to live with little. Eventually they found a rental. It was on a busy street and its floors were dark. No sunlight came through the windows because of a cherry tree, and the roar of the cars sounded like an angry cat's hiss. This made her think of Henry, who disappeared. She sometimes picked green cherries off the tree and peeled them, wondering whether she would ever hold them in her hand when they were ripe, perplexed at how little she cared. She wondered about the beans, if they had grown. But she never went back to the garden beds to gather produce, and the only time she entered the backyard was to look for Henry.

People were generous. They raised money for them, brought them platters of macaroni and cheese, salmon, and ripe tomatoes from their gardens. The only thing she couldn't stand was being told to be grateful.

"You are so lucky, really," said Kate when she visited with a pineapple and flowers.

It was the first day they had the rental, a small house with gray floors and a black table and no beds yet. "I guess," said Joan, looking at Kate's chiseled face and hating her.

One day she was poring through insurance documents, scanning the pictures of all their lost belongings and estimating their prices, looking in horror at the picture of Jeremy's room black and gray with the light hanging from an electric wire, the bed gone, the desk gone, the floors charred, *As if It Never Happened* written above the photo. The doorbell rang.

Joan opened the door to a woman from the neighborhood, and she said, "Clover! So glad to see you."

Clover was a nonfiction writer with long, dark hair and a silver pendant who wrote about the spiritual side of things, and her logo on her card read "Walk in Grace," a woman with a rainbow twirling from her hand. Joan didn't really know her at all, had met her once at the park. "I bought you macaroni and cheese, gluten and dairy free. I thought you could use some comfort food."

Joan took the platter and Clover followed her in and added to her gifts a tiny cactus plant, which she set on the table. "And a plant," she said. "I'm so sorry about what you're going through, but you are really so lucky you're alive."

Joan sat at the table and rubbed her forehead. "Yeah, I guess."

Clover reached out for her hand and looked earnestly in her eyes. "And just think of all the refugees in other countries who don't even have a bed to sleep in, or people dying of starvation. You are truly blessed and will grow from this," she said.

Joan didn't know that two years later the Amazon would burn, that the investment firms for cattle ranching in Brazil had the mega-donors of her president and the Senate majority leader, that in order to slaughter more cattle to eat, rainforests would turn into savannahs, that fire was far worse when it took down the lungs of the earth. But she didn't want to know how tiny her experience was, how trivial when her world had fallen apart.

She leaned back and looked at Clover's flowing pink shirt. "I know Jeremy, if he had been in his room, would have put out the fire or gotten away. It was the incense. I don't think we were in danger. Well, I guess Michele was because she was in the studio and for some reason didn't notice the smoke." Joan blinked and rubbed her temples. She was so tired of cogitating about the what ifs.

Clover looked at Joan as if her thinking was beside the point. "Yes, but fire is dangerous and your family has overcome it."

Joan glanced down at the picture of Jeremy's room. It was blurry and black and gray. The light hung from his ceiling, broken. "Have we?" she asked, then shrugged.

Clover left, and Joan texted Alyssa.

People keep telling me to be grateful and I'm not.

Alyssa texted back, *You be as pissed as you want, girl. You're a badass.*

Joan looked at the bare white walls of the rental and the cactus on the table, adorned with thorns. She didn't want to be grateful. Not yet. Not when she'd lost her home, and the rental felt alien to her, its gray carpet foreign under her feet, its thermostat confounding. Not when the nightmares of scarred flesh and lost children haunted her, and her mother was dying, and all she wanted now was her mother to lean on, to pick her up as she fell.

Joan of Arc

After the fire, Joan received a post from Next Door about free kittens. Looking at the picture of the five kittens lying peacefully next to their black mother, Joan thought about Henry, who she still hadn't found, and decided she would adopt some. And her mutt, Filbert, a mix of cattle dog, Border Collie, Labrador, and God knows what, was great with cats. She picked them up from a kind old man who wore red-checkered slippers and smiled at her warmly. He handed her one kitten after another, and Joan pet the smooth black one and decided she would name it Midnight. The other one was Spot.

Joan felt like Noah saving the animals from the flood. After the fire they'd had no clothes, no toothbrushes, no bed to return to. The hotel smelled like air freshener. The rental was so foreign still. She never knew where anything was. She would open up cabinet after cabinet to find plates. She made salad in a large pot, her salad bowl painted with sunflowers gone. She felt like everything she'd been able to supply for the family was gone. That plate a friend of Darren's had made for their wedding, and the clothes she'd worn, well, they hadn't been important, but the leather jacket she'd bought in a Berlin flea market had been precious to her. It had so many zippers. Joan liked zippers, how they closed pockets. Her life was a scattering.

When she arrived home with the kittens and cat food, the expensive kind that used organic chicken even though they were broke, Darren was at the kitchen table putting together documents for the insurance company. He lifted his head, looked at the kittens, and said, "Joan, for God's sake." He sighed.

"Now that Henry is gone, we should give a home to something else that needs it," she said, pleading.

"We signed a contract that says, 'No Cats'," said Darren. "Dammit, Joan."

Spot began scratching on the rental's blue couch and ripped lines across its plush surface, and Midnight lunged at Darren's toes.

"What happened to that pink plastic bowl? We could put the water in it." Joan brushed the hair out of her eyes and began rummaging through the cabinets with the handful of dishes they bought after the fire. They only had four bowls for the family, but she decided she'd just use a coffee mug for the tomatillo soup she would warm for dinner. Motherhood was sacrifice. She didn't need a damn bowl.

Darren yelled, "Shit," and kicked Midnight off his leg, where three thin scratches bloomed blood. Spot went to the carpet and started kneading, then pissed.

"Oops, I forgot to buy a litter box." Joan found a mixing bowl and poured cat litter into it and lifted Spot. She put him in it and he knocked it over. The litter spilled on the floor.

The next week she bought birds at Petco, chose them from a huge cage set in the middle of the store, parakeets blue and green that she named Pan and Bitsy. Her teenage children were playing with the kittens on the kitchen floor, and Joan set the cage with the parakeets on the table and said, "Look what I got!"

But the children remained indifferent to the birds, and though beautiful, they were noisy and covered the floor with seed and feathers, and the kittens would jump on the counter and try to knock the cage over. One day Midnight decided to lunge his whole body at the cage, and it fell. Pan and Bitsy flew across the living room and landed on the T.V. While flinging himself against the television screen as he flew up to try to catch one, Spot tumbled on the floor and meowed loudly.

Michele was reading a book and yelled, "Mom, Pan is pooping on the carpet. And aren't we supposed to clip their wings?" she asked.

"Birds are meant to fly. That would be cruel."

"Mom, they're supposed to live in cages," Michele reminded her.

Joan began to sweep up the birdseed and wipe down the spilled water. "Maybe we should put rocks in the cage to make it heavier so it won't fall." She looked out the window at the pebble-strewn square outside their house that wasn't their home. Gathering a handful of pebbles, she thought about how amazing water was, how it can crumble mountains into small stones. She was thirsty. She came back into the house to pour herself a glass of water, but they had no glasses, so she found a coffee mug that said *I Love New York* on it that she'd found at Goodwill, but it was crusty with last night's dinner of barbeque pork, so she stuck her head in the sink and drank out of the tap.

Joan locked the kittens in the bathroom and spent an hour coaxing the birds back into the cage, now filled with gray stones. Pan had somehow lost his blue tail feather, which shimmered and made Joan think of the sea. She put it in the vase with the sage she had collected to purify the house of ghosts.

When Joan brought home the gerbils, which she named Sam and Artie, her family confronted her.

"Honey," said Darren while rummaging through his wallet, "this pet business is getting out of hand."

"But Michele has always wanted a gerbil!"

Michele was on their black couch clipping her nails. She raised her head and looked at Joan, exasperated and rolling her eyes. "Mom, I was six years old then. I'm sixteen now."

Jeremy came into the room from the basement and peered down at the gerbils and asked, "Where do gerbils actually come from? Do they live wild somewhere?"

Joan thought about it and decided she would just say Australia, because it seemed like if they had kangaroos, they probably had gerbils, too. "Australia," she said with conviction.

Joan looked in the aquarium, where one of the gerbils was running on its wheel. The kittens were swatting at the glass walls, and then Midnight jumped on top of the aquarium and peered down and scratched at the screen, looking hungry. Joan went outside and collected more pebbles and set them on the bottom of the aquarium to make the aquarium heavier, then rummaged for string to tie it closed.

The day the landlord from California called, she had just brought home a snake. Her landlord was only a voice to her, and they conducted all their business via email or phone. The snake writhed and slept in the aquarium and ate mice she bought frozen because now she was getting attached to Sam and Artie, who were soft and furry to the touch and had perfect, small black eyes, and Joan decided she loved rodents. But then one morning she awoke and the snake was gone. She called his name, Lezane, which means "loved one," because she had decided she would also love the snake even though it wasn't furry and didn't seem to do much except wrap itself around Jeremy's body when he showed it to friends, its triangular head swaying near his neck like the rhythm of waves, which made her think of her landlord in LA and wonder if he surfed. She searched behind the couch and under the beds. She pulled all the clothes out of the hamper and even looked in the washer and dryer.

When the landlord called, he asked, "How's it going?"

"Oh, great," said Joan. "But the window shades in the living room broke." Midnight and Spot had torn them apart with their sharp claws.

"No problem. We'll fix them when we come to Colorado this fall."

Joan liked her landlord. All landlords should live in California, she thought. They could surf on the Pacific waves while she claimed her new home.

A week later it turned out that Sam the gerbil was actually a Samantha, and the cage was full of squirming pink babies. Joan thought they were cute, but Jeremy said that maybe they should feed them to Lezane if they ever found him.

But Samantha was a bad mother. Before her babies could open their eyes, Samantha ate them all. One day they were writhing in the cedar chips, and the next they were simply gone.

Joan looked at the bags of cedar chips, the scattered seed, the blue feathers, the granules of cat litter on the wood floor, and listened to the cacophony of bird song, which sometimes sounded like sirens.

The Decisions

After four months of living in the rental, acquiring clothes, and collecting their menagerie of pets, Joan, Darren, and the kids finally moved back into the house. Joan was so sick of probation, but she had become used to sobriety and her bitchy probation officer, Angela, a woman with a mouth like a torn fingernail and stringy hair and full of threats.

One morning in late August, two weeks after they had moved back in, Joan was vacuuming the floors in the kids' bedrooms while Michele rode her bike to work and Jeremy and Darren had left to work on the house, and it was so hot that she drank a gallon of water. She called in and it was a test day, and the next day she was called into the office because she tested diluted.

Angela sat behind a cluttered desk above blue stained carpet, behind her a window looking out to a parking lot and Arapahoe Street. She placed her fists on the table and said, "You tested positive and if it happens again, you're going to jail."

Joan felt fear well in her stomach and said, "How can that be? I haven't drunk anything but water!"

Angela frowned, her thin mouth tight, then said, "We consider testing diluted positive."

After that, Joan made sure not to drink too much water during a test day and put creatine powder in her water on the days she was tested.

Now Joan was home again. The lucky dinosaur fossil remained at her side the whole time. When they'd been allowed into the house, she took it, and it smelled like smoke, but she knew that would fade in time. In the rental she kept it under the mattress where she slept, and now home she put it back in the cabinet of her bedside table, where it had been before. Darren had replaced the floors and windows, painted the walls, and the house, after almost two decades of kids and smudges and scratches, looked and felt like new. In some ways, Joan felt reborn. It was a return but also coming home to something new.

However, in the midst of the homecoming, Joan's mother was not doing well. Joan still visited her every day, but she also spent time picking up phone calls from Into the Light about something that had happened. Jim wasn't there anymore. He had been fired. A caretaker told her it was because he was accused of stealing the residents' drugs.

Sometimes Joan wished she hadn't volunteered to take her mother's care into her own hands. Her sister Angelika hadn't offered. Joan and Angelika were estranged since Angelika had voted for Trump the year before, and they never spoke. She lived in South Carolina with a black servant and no children, and she and her husband always traveled to Greece, where they owned a villa.

Joan wasn't working at this time, still on summer vacation from the college where she taught composition. One of her favorite pastimes was shopping for clothes, since she had lost so many in the fire.

Joan found the boutique one day when she took a wrong turn. She ended up on a street with car dealerships and nestled between two of them was a tiny boutique called Rags to Riches, where she found a blue velvet dress with silver buttons, soft to the touch like a cat's fur. She bought it.

Of all the decisions she had to make, those concerning her poor mother were the worst. Her mother's Alzheimer's had eaten her brain, and her mother babbled nonsense that everyone thought was German. They would say to Joan, "Your mother is so sweet. I just wish I understood German!" Joan would smile, even though the language had about as much German as the night had light—smidgeons of it in headlights, the ones that came to you, a stray word like *haben* or *wo*, have or where, nothing you could follow. No destination. And yet that was the torturous situation Joan was always in—trying to understand her mother—what she needed, how she was feeling. Joan felt completely at a loss when she had to decide anything for her mother, like whether to let the ambulance take her to the hospital.

One day while they were still in the rental, Joan was visiting a doctor friend, Jason, in the suburbs, enjoying a glass of white wine and gazing at their lilac bush.

Jason was standing at the sink in his suit. He turned to her and asked, "How's your mother doing?"

"She's fine, as fine as you can be when you've lost so many brain cells," Joan said.

Jason held up a hand in a gesture that Joan normally associated with someone who was asking you to stop. "Just make sure she never ends up in a hospital."

"Why?" Joan asked.

"Because they are miserable, scared, and confused. They need to stay in their home."

Joan always remembered that conversation. Her mother's little world offered her security.

And in that home, her mother was a very busy woman. Many of the residents just sat and watched TV or stared into space. Her mother walked hunched through the hallways, went into everyone's rooms, approached residents eating in the dining room and stole their food, and caused so much chaos the caregivers begged the doctor to give her more drugs, but they did little to lessen her agitation.

So one day her mother got hold of a bottle of lemon dish soap, drank it all, and had explosive diarrhea. They called the paramedics who called Joan while she was folding laundry. They wanted to take her to the hospital. Joan folded a green towel.

"Absolutely not," she said.

The second time her mother had fallen in the courtyard after tripping on a pot of petunias and cut her head.

When they called her, Joan was cutting onions and crying. She asked if the wound was deep and whether it needed stitches. "Probably not," they said, so she replied, "Then don't take her to the hospital, please," but they did, insisting it was the only way to get the wound properly bandaged. Between the ambulance ride and the treatment, that bill took Joan six months to pay.

The third time, her mother had an inflamed left cheek, bulbous and swollen as if she carried a tennis ball in her mouth. Joan had a geriatric dentist come, who said they would need to extract four of her teeth. Joan agreed. She visited her mother that evening and her mouth was still swollen and she couldn't eat. The next day she wouldn't get out of bed.

Then the decision was whether to take her to a hospital and put her on an antibiotic I.V. or leave her as she was in her small room in the home.

Joan thought of her mother's life—the hikes through the Alps in Austria, the protesting of Vietnam, the years teaching languages in high school, her voluble and passionate conversations with people. Now she couldn't speak, could barely walk, and rarely smiled anymore. Joan said no to antibiotics altogether. It was like teaching her teenagers to drive—that letting go, that releasing into the unknown from a decision at once sharp and opaque.

Joan put her mother in hospice. Her mother lived another ten days. It was not a pretty death. She sweated and fought with ragged breaths. Joan begged hospice for more morphine. Finally they agreed, and then her mother died. Joan called Angelika who said it was a blessing. They didn't have a memorial.

Now Joan's decisions are much easier.

She finds joy in having to choose between roast beef or chicken for dinner, whether a student deserves a B or B+, or whether to buy caramel or chocolate. She decides whether to wear her brown boots with buckles or her black Doc Martins. She decides who to vote for, which brand of face cream to buy, and whether to bring kale salad or chile to potlucks. She decides what to wear to weddings or memorials.

Sometimes when the season moves into autumn, she thinks of her mother in the funeral home. Her face was gaunt, the swelling of her mouth gone, and her skin was the color of parchment, dry and wrinkled like an autumn leaf. She imagined now her mother was wandering in the sky, speaking fluent German to God, wearing the velvet blue dress that Joan had chosen especially for her.

The Hermit

Joan was convinced she had cancer ever since she turned forty-seven. Sometimes it was a dull ache in her side, sometimes a cut that didn't heal. She knew of a woman with breast cancer who died after saying no to a mastectomy and going to Mexico instead for herbal treatments, and just recently an old friend of hers died of pancreatic cancer. It was just a matter of time before those alien cells took over her body. Her body was on the edge of a cliff, ready to fall. When she got out her Tarot deck, she always drew the Fool. Once she saw the Hermit in a dream. He dropped his lantern and the light tumbled down into a rocky canyon, glowing on the silver cliffs as it fell. It was winter, with pockets of snow on the peaks.

It was winter again in the real world and Joan was swimming three days a week, teaching composition, and training dogs because it was a good side job and she'd got certified years ago, and she preferred it to writing food reviews, which she stopped doing. She was trying unsuccessfully to wrangle her unruly children, Jeremy a junior now and Michele a sophomore. The children were tracking mud in the house, driving in the snow, and staying for the most part invisible except when they were hungry. Once she'd let them have a party, and after Joan had passed out at midnight, the kids smoked weed and drank. The next day Joan had to deal with an irate mother, who came over to lecture her. The other mom said she picked up her daughter puking on their lawn when she'd come to pick her up. Joan wondered whether puke was good for the soil.

One day after a grueling day of swimming, where she barreled through a series of 100s that just about killed her, she walked into the house and saw a bottle of glue on the table. She thought it strange. And yet, her teenage children had been acting especially odd lately—sniffing a lot and saying it was a cold. She knew she was a bad mother. Jeremy was flunking pre-calculus, and Michele wore lace bras that stuck out of her shirts and her neck was always adorned with hickies. She thought about their waggish attitude and dismissive excuses of just having too much homework. They either diverted or rolled their eyes when she talked to them. When she kissed their messy heads, they turned away from her. She decided her teenage children were sniffing glue, and this time she would be a better mother and do something about it.

That evening at dinner, the sun was waning through their windows, and the dying orchid above the kitchen sink on the windowsill was blooming. She looked at all the abundance of purple candles and oak floors and willow branches climbing, and she thought about what a contrast it was to their life. She was dying of cancer. And yes, she realized, her children were sniffing glue. She pressed her eyeballs, so round and delicate under those thin lids, and it occurred to her that if it weren't for the turpitude and moral depravity of her children, the world would be a better place.

Finally, she pushed a potato on the side of her plate and sighed. "Michele, Jeremy, what's this about the glue?"

Jeremy sat behind his plate of fried steak and mushrooms and asked, "What glue?"

"I mean the glue on the counter."

"I don't know," he said.

"Mom, weren't you cleaning out that drawer with all our old school supplies?" Michele asked.

Joan didn't remember putting anything on the counter. She had been distracted before leaving to swim. She'd just returned from a new job training two young huskies. Their owner was a glass artist, with sculptures of red camels, murals of the rainforest women with long black hair with toucans on their shoulders, abstract pieces of blue swirls embedded in clear glass. His dogs were named Loki and Freya, and he talked about mythology and the tree of life. He showed her a sculpture of Odin with a patch across his eye and a cane. The dogs were beautiful, like wolves. Loki had blue eyes, and Freya's eyes were ebony. Joan worked on sit and down with them, but they weren't interested in her treats. She knew from her training as a dog trainer that praise was sometimes enough, so she praised them lavishly, and they sauntered away from her, sniffed each other's noses, and plunged their faces into her crotch. She needed to find treats that worked.

At the dinner table, Joan eyed her daughter, this soon-to-be woman who looked so much like she did once, without the red hair, and knew she couldn't be trusted. She saw the blood vessels reddened on the whites of Michele's eyes, the way they complemented the mouth bruises on her throat. And now Jeremy was staring out of the window with his mouth open, his fork jammed with a huge hunk of food in his hand because he was obviously so high that he'd forgotten how to cut. She went to bed and couldn't sleep, though she had one fitful dream of letting Jeremy drive, but he refused to take the wheel, and the car careened toward a cliff.

The next day she returned from buying Jeremy socks, and there was another bottle of glue, this time in Jeremy's room in the dresser drawer where she put his socks. Joan opened it and took a big sniff. It didn't really smell like much. She sniffed again, as deeply as she could, then brought the bottle downstairs and poured the glue on a paper towel and inhaled with her mouth, then deeply with her nose, but still it failed to make her high. The kids must be mixing it with something, so she looked up how to get high on glue. She watched videos of children in South Africa reeling and falling on the dirt with cloudy bottles of it in their hands. She watched a mother of two strolling down the dirt streets in a shanty town, everything bathed in dust, collecting money to feed her children by selling bottles of glue. She found out that it needed to be industrial glue.

She walked downstairs and opened the door to the garage and peered at all the cans on the shelves. Surely one of them was industrial glue. Finally on the bottom shelf she found a can of furniture glue behind Jeremy's bike hung on the ceiling. She pushed the wheel aside and it hit her in the back as she approached the can, surrounded by cans of paint and lacquer. It was already partly pried open. Yes, the kids were sniffing glue.

She needed to figure out what they were doing to their minds. She pulled off the top and inhaled it deeply and felt dizzy, light-headed, and slightly nauseous. Her brain felt like it was on fire, and she saw another image of The Hermit from the dream. This time his lantern shined a red light that swirled into a rose as she closed her eyes.

When she found her balance, she came into the house and read about The Hermit. It was the ancient spirit that represents the deepest part of her, knows what to do, how to respond to the world, an indication that one should find the answers within oneself. Joan needed to follow her own intuition.

That evening before making dinner, she did some more research on glue sniffing and it was harrowing. Children holding broken bottles to their noses in Africa. Brain damage. Death. Joan realized that she had been so concerned lately about her own impending death that she had failed to see that her children were killing themselves.

When they sat down to dinner, Joan decided to take a more indirect approach. As her husband and Jeremy scrolled on their phones and Michele plunged her fork into the chicken as if killing it, Joan again said, "So, what's this with the glue?"

Michele was the only one listening. Darren and Jeremy were texting, their faces plastered on their phones. She said, "What glue?"

"Jeremy, I found glue in your room," she said. Jeremy stared at his phone and laughed. She leaned over and tapped him on the shoulder. "Jeremy, what's with the glue?"

He lifted his head and ran his hand through his greasy hair. "What glue?"

"The glue I found in your room!"

"I don't know, maybe I should clean my room."

"Maybe?" Darren said, returning long enough from his text to pretend to think this family discussion was about chores before he then returned to his phone.

"What about the open can in the garage?" Joan asked.

"What are you talking about?" Michele looked at her as if exhausted.

Joan looked at the rings under Michele's eyes, stamped her foot down and yelled, "You two are sniffing glue!"

Both her children looked up at her and rolled their eyes. Michele pushed aside her Brussel sprouts and said, "Mom, we're not sniffing glue."

Joan needed some support. "Darren," she said to her husband, "Can you tell the children not to sniff glue?"

Darren glanced up and said, "What's that?"

"Can you tell the kids to stop sniffing glue?" Joan felt like crying. She felt a burning in her gut. It was probably stomach cancer.

Darren sighed and turned to them and said, "Stop sniffing glue."

When she'd been a teenager, she would go to the local fair in the parking lot of K-Mart and smoke bowls of Thai stick. She'd vomited on roller coasters just to eat mushrooms at a friend's house an hour afterward. She'd wandered on train tracks, balancing on the iron and stumbling onto the wooden ties to laugh until the moon had descended into her eyes, and she still wasn't blind like she wanted to be. She had to always see the ugly world with its slums and dying trees and suffering.

Joan was training the huskies again. Because they didn't seem treat-oriented, Joan brought slices of raw steak. The man was in the basement blowing glass, and she spent the time in the living room helping them with their new skills. Freya licked her hand when Joan told her to "leave it," and Loki lay on his brown dog bed looking bored before Joan brought out the bloody steak, and then he barely gave her a nod when she'd asked him to sit.

The only problem was the huskies liked the steak a lot after they'd had a taste. In fact, they were so excited by it that when Joan was working on recall, standing in front of a table with the red glass camel, the dogs came bounding toward her. She lost her balance and reeled into the table, and the red camel tumbled and shattered on the floor. Freya flew across the room and barreled into the sofa, yelping, and limped away.

When the man emerged from the basement, Joan explained that the Huskies were adolescent, and because they were huskies, they were more genetically related to wolves. She pulled at a red thread from the leash and looked at a glass sculpture of two women entwined with a tree.

"They're wild," she said.

The man rubbed his gray beard, then he rubbed his belly. He looked up at the ceiling.

"I'm sorry." Joan picked at her cuticles, nervous, and fleetingly thinking how she would die.

"God, maybe I took off more than I can chew with these huskies." The man frowned.

"Well, huskies are challenging. They're made to pull sleds. Do you have a sled?"

"No, but I hike."

"Okay, but keep them on a leash. Huskies aren't good off leash."

Joan's cuticle started to bleed. She put her finger in her mouth and tasted the metallic blood.

When she returned home, she decided to excavate the laundry room, which was filled with old mops and dusty rags. She opened up a cabinet and found three bottles of glue. She collected all the glue in the house and threw it away, thinking that there might be a way the kids were getting high on it, and then she went into the garage and contemplated how to get rid of the can. She picked it up. It was cold and heavy. What exactly were the kids feeling when they sniffed glue? She thought she should try it again so that she could understand. She took another sniff out of the can and fell back against the car.

Her mind was turning in circles, and when she closed her eyes, she felt a ray of light ascend from her forehead. She saw an image of her father flying out of a window holding a lantern of red light. She heard sirens. She leaned against the car and then tried to stand, but the bicycle tire hit her in the cheek, so she rested back against the car's door. After a few minutes, she decided to hide the can behind the leaf blower and cover it with a tarp. Now the kids wouldn't find it.

She walked into the house and opened her computer to watch more videos about glue sniffing. One little boy, flies circling and landing on his face, said that sniffing glue made life much more bearable since he needed to eat garbage, and glue sniffing was a motivator to eat garbage when nothing else worked. He was squatting with two other boys on a red dirt road, the background of thatch-roofed huts and strewn plastic bottles.

She decided to become a better cook. She would make a soufflé that evening. She pored through *The Joy of Cooking* but realized she had no milk so used water instead. The dinner left puddles on their plates and the soggy eggs crumbled. Joan sighed as she ate with her family at the dinner table and they said nothing. People just wanted to escape all the time, she thought to herself. Who could blame them? With all the cancer, dying bees, general inertia of humans to find a remedy for this godforsaken world, and the horrific planet destruction, who could blame them? A fire in California burned every home in a town called Paradise and left over eighty people dead. The Supreme Court was rigged. Her children were drug addicts, and she was dying of cancer.

Joan leaned over her husband's shoulder and kissed his face while she and her children were dying. Darren kissed her cheek. Jeremy was scrolling on his phone and Michele was mutilating her soufflé, crumbling the watery eggs adorning her plate. Joan felt a pang in her gut and fleetingly contemplated whether she had colon cancer. Tears welled in her eyes. Her children were young and deserved to live long lives after she died. Now poor Darren would lose his family, and he would have to find another wife, and she would probably already have children whom he couldn't bond with, and every night he would weep and think of Joan's beautiful curves, and the days they brought home their newborns wrapped in blankets and she nursing them on soft pillows.

"Kids," she said, tapping Jeremy on the shoulder, "This glue sniffing has got to stop."

"We're not sniffing glue!" yelled Michele.

"You are! It's a horrible, horrible drug. It ruins your brain and kills you. I'd rather you do crack."

Jeremy tapped his finger on the table. "Mom, crack is so eighties, people do meth now."

"Well, meth is better than glue."

Michele said, "So you're telling us to do meth?"

"No, we spend enough on the dentist already!" Joan tapped Darren's shoulder. He was immersed in his phone, his dinner untouched. "Tell them I'm not telling them to do meth."

Darren lifted his head. "What's that?"

"Tell them I'm not telling them to do meth."

Darren said, "Mom's saying not to do meth." He looked at his phone. "Hey, Jeremy, check out this video."

Jeremy leaned over Darren's shoulder. Joan looked at it and saw a crowd of people in a marathon running. They were covered in sweat and wearing numbers.

Darren pointed at a stick-like figure and said, "This Kenyon man won."

Joan hollered, "And in Kenya people are dying from sniffing glue!"

Michele slammed her hand on the table and said, "Oh my God, Mom," and left.

The next day Joan found the perfect treats for Loki and Freya, and she decided to work outside on leash this time. She leashed both the dogs and held them close, carefully walking around a glass blue horse. She put them on a heel as she walked past a pink and orange figure of a pregnant woman. They stepped out of the house and walked a block away and did a sit stay. She moved to the end of the leash. They looked into her eyes and Joan felt a strong connection, a bond as if she were from the same litter, and she was the alpha dog, directing the pack. When she looked into Loki's blue eyes, she saw the sky, and when she looked into Freya's, she saw the black night. The three of them together contained the world. After three successful tries, when the dogs sat still for her and waited, she decided to drop the leashes and walk farther away.

The dogs bolted. Joan ran toward them with strips of steak dangling from her hands, but they were off, careening around the neighbor's house. She slipped on some ice while looking at a perfectly swept patio and a chiminea in someone's backyard. The house was blue. She ran past many houses that seemed uninhabited, with perfect lawns, not a person in sight, just occasional movement of the two dogs running away, their bodies like streaks of gray light. Then nothing but the houses; the dogs had disappeared.

She walked to the house and went to the basement. The man was surrounded by glass sculptures of what looked like gnomes, small pudgy men with blue hats. In the corner was a stove, and ashes covered the concrete floor below it. The man was listening to classical music and leaning forward, writing a check. She nudged him. He turned to her and for a moment he looked like he didn't recognize her. He set down his pen.

"The dogs have gotten loose," she said.

The man rubbed his chin, his hands red from all the glass and fire.

"You're fired," he said.

Joan drove home. She wanted a shot of whiskey. She sat in the kitchen and contemplated what leftovers she could feed the kids, then decided she could reheat the strips of steak for the dogs and mix it with the leftover crumbly soufflé. It could be a kind of stir fry.

Jeremy came into the kitchen. "Mom, I need glue for a project for Spanish."

Joan sighed. "We're all out of glue."

That evening she snuck into the garage while Darren was watching a football game and the kids were at a party. She pushed the leaf blower aside. She pulled the tarp off the can. She circled its edge with her fingers, the cold metal as smooth as the ice on their driveway, and pried it open. She put her face down and inhaled deeply until the light shined behind her closed eyes and she fell against the car again. It reminded her of how much she'd always loved the smell of gas when she filled her car, that chemical smell similar, which she could taste in her mouth. She thought about The Hermit, how alone he was on the barren mountain. The lantern lit the way for The Fool to see the edge. He would watch his feet as he danced off the cliff. Her head swirled and she saw a carousel with horses adorned with golden saddles. She saw wolves running in the mountains, crashing through pine. She reeled back onto the car and then fell on the concrete floor. She felt her body dying into the light outside of the dark garage, becoming the wild wolves, hunting.

Joan Ponders Spit

It was Christmas day, so Joan was bored.

Her children had already opened their presents. Michele cried because she hadn't gotten enough to open, although she had specifically said all she wanted was cash. Jeremy was grateful for the socks. Darren frowned at his presents and announced he would return them all, which happened every year, but this time Joan thought she really got it right with the blue rain jacket from REI. Apparently, he didn't like the zippers.

Then there was a late breakfast and nothing to do but look online for apartments to rent.

Not that Joan was going to move out, especially after living in the awful rental after the fire; it was just something she liked to fantasize about: living alone in a cozy apartment, writing poetry and taking walks, bringing a lover, a big man like Jim, to her space with art on the walls and warm feather blankets. In any case, she lived in Boulder, so whenever she looked for a place, her dreams were shattered. The apartments were either ridiculously expensive or they insisted on "no pets, no drugs." Life would be hard enough without her pets, which she enjoyed because of their general furriness and inability to talk back at her. She loved her dog, cats, and birds, and maybe could give them up, but no drugs? They lived in Colorado, for God's sake, where marijuana was legal! And eventually she would be off probation and Lord knows she'd be smoking weed. So finding a dream apartment became a hopeless task.

After discarding all the wrapper covered in reindeer and snowmen, they decided to watch an episode of *Outlander*, about a woman who travels through time to 18th century Scotland, falls in love with a handsome Scot, tries to change history by influencing a war, heals the wounded, gives birth to a stillborn baby, and loves and mourns and fights for their lives with passion. Joan loved the show. It was just like her life. But the show's season was over, and they would have to pay for another season, so they decided to watch a documentary about caves instead.

Jeremy was devouring a bag of potato chips and said, "This is so cool, don't you think?"

Joan watched in awe and disgust as a glowworm in a cave in Borneo excreted mucous that descended in a thin line to catch insects. When the glowworm caught the bug, it sucked up all the mucous until it reached the bug and consumed it, wings and all.

"How can it even have room to eat the bug if it has to eat all the mucous?" Joan asked. She did not enjoy dealing with her own spit and mucous, an often inconvenient excretion of her body that poured out of her when she was cold, and worms just grossed her out in general with their thin long digestive tracts—apparently full of mucous—and their slimy, pink-white bodies.

"Look at the lit-up lines dangling from the ceiling though, Mom, isn't it beautiful?"

Darren was silent and Michele upstairs, so Joan had no support in her suggestion that the world of the cave was exceedingly gross. She didn't want to invalidate her son's experience, though. "I guess." They kind of looked like Christmas lights, and since it was Christmas, she should be positive. Then she couldn't resist. "But Jeremy, it's a glowing line of mucous!"

"Oh, Mom, you're just being all cooty-like."

Then they showed a section about a kind of swallow that lives in those abominable caves. The swallow builds a nest out of its spit. It can take up to thirty days to create their special white nests that sit on the cave's black wall. Unfortunately, the nests are in demand for an ingredient in bird's nest soup in Asia, so people descend into the caves with ladders made of rope and vines and steal them.

"More spit! I guess part of survival in living in a cave is to be creative with your spit," exclaimed Joan.

"Mom, Jeez." Jeremy sighed. "Dad, maybe we could go spelunking one day."

Darren grunted. He was on his phone on the couch.

When they showed a segment about swarms of cockroaches that lived on gigantic piles of bat shit and consumed both the feces and the poor occasional bat that fell on the pile, voraciously eating it alive to the skeleton, Joan couldn't take it anymore. She got up, looked at the clock, decided 3:00 p.m. was too early for the martini she craved, and she couldn't drink one anyway, and made herself some green tea.

That evening she thought of the poor swallows. They spent so much time making their nests, gave of their body to build a home and a cradle for their children, then it was all taken from them in a day. She thought about starting over, how she too was always starting over. Every day she accomplished and failed at the same tasks— teaching, cooking, cleaning, training, shopping. At night her cave grew dark, and she erased the day in sleep and dreams, and the next day she did it again, like the birds with their saliva after their homes became someone's dinner.

But it was different because she had her home. She would be like Batwoman and fight for the swallows, fight for her cave, defend the weak and live in her dark stone home that survived even when it defied any light. She would savor it all—even her precious spit.

But she still liked to look at apartments for rent. Just because. So she crept upstairs to the master bedroom where she curled up on the bed, under the covers, and opened Zillow instead of Craig's List because the apartments were nicer. She coveted a studio in the Mapleton neighborhood with French doors for $3,500 a month. The apartment in South Boulder was also lovely, with a large deck in the back where she could grill chicken and watch the sun set over the mountains and know, sleeping soundly, alone, in bed, that it would rise in the morning just for her.

The Painted Wall

Joan couldn't stand her neighbors. How she ended up in the suburbs was beyond her. The men all worked for Google or insurance companies and were gone all day, leaving at 6:00 a.m. in their Audis, the women remaining behind to prune their roses, or play tennis, staying at home so they could concern themselves with things like other people's dogs.

Her neighbors Kate and Spencer were the worst. They were uptight poor-turned-rich Republicans with two children they helicopter-parented to the point where both children were shells of human beings and cold as dead trout. Joan and Darren were rich-turned-poor Democrats. But Darren liked Kate because of their connection with sports, so Joan hated her even more than all the other neighbors.

She had learned a valuable lesson about neighbors when she'd lived in Berlin in 1987, that city with the gorgeous wall covered in art: you can always try to cross the border.

Joan had lived in the Kreuzberg District of West Berlin for a summer two years before she married Darren, along the Paul Linke Ufer where a green canal meandered next to the wall with a view of gray buildings and dark windows of East Berlin. Every day she would smoke cigarettes with her cousin Katharina and talk about astrology, America's Wild West, and beer.

Katharina had grown up in East Berlin and escaped over the wall in a hot air balloon and now cleaned a neighborhood bar and lived in dire poverty. In her tiny apartment she painted cowboys, horses, and Indians. She had never been to America. After visiting Katharina, Joan would ride her bike to the Mexican restaurant where she worked as a cook with other foreigners, and when she received her cash, she spent it on beer as she flirted in bars all night, played pool, and slam-danced. Then she would sleep in and start the whole routine again.

Joan worried about Katharina. She had nobody in her life. Her father was dead and her mother lived across the border in the East. All Katharina had were images from movies and fantasies about America that she spent the day painting. Often Joan felt angry at her aunt for choosing ideology over relationship. Because her Aunt Ursula had dual citizenship, she could live in the West if she wanted, but she was an avid communist.

One day, when Joan was sitting under a weeping willow along the canal and looking at a section of the wall painted with *Make Love Not Wall*, Joan planned her Tuesday off from work. She would visit her Aunt Ursula in East Berlin, who was a drug addict with hair a deep rust color that was the trend in Germany. The last time they talked, Ursula asked her to bring bottle openers, so Joan had bought ten of them. She also bought her a necklace with a stone ram pendant, since her aunt was an Aries.

The next morning, Joan took the Friedrichstrasse U-Bahn to the border. In the gray and dark underground train stop, a drunk woman slept on the wooden bench with a bottle of schnaps and an old man asked Joan for cigarettes. Joan gave him three and climbed the stairs to the checkpoint.

Three border guards sat behind a white table and Joan approached them. They were wearing green uniforms and smoking, and behind them was an open door revealing an empty metal desk. A guard with black hair peeking out of his hat and a shadow of a beard motioned for her to sit down across from him.

"Are you bringing any presents for your aunt?" he asked as Joan sat down on the plastic chair.

Joan looked at his yellow teeth and green uniform and squirmed.

"Just a few," she said.

"Let me have your backpack."

Joan handed her bag to him, and he rummaged through it. He took out the bottle openers, necklace, and journal.

"Your aunt is a lucky woman." He smiled, but it didn't reach his eyes. "You like to visit your aunt? You like our country?"

"I've never been there before." Joan glanced at the exit, impatient. "I'm sure it's nice," Joan lied in her halting German.

"Where are you from?"

Although Joan was fluent in German, she had an accent. She didn't want to say America, especially not to communist guards, so she lied. "Canada," she said.

"Lots of trees in Canada, huh?" he said. He looked down at her bag.

He opened her journal and started writing the names and contact information of her friends that she kept on the last page. Joan felt as if he was splitting her open and taking a part of her.

He took nine of the bottle openers and let her keep one. "Your aunt only needs one of these," he said.

East Berlin was as gray as the rats she saw every night in the West. The buildings were concrete blocks with windows, and streets empty of people. Next to her aunt's apartment building was a playground on a concrete slab with one rusty swing set and a slide. Joan could have sworn the day had been sunny before she had descended underground, but now the sky was gray with either smoke or clouds, and the buildings were covered with streaks of black.

Her aunt, wearing a polyester white dress, her purple-red hair in a bun, hugged her as she entered the tiny apartment. The kitchen had a tiny plastic table surrounded by plastic red chairs, and there was not one cushioned piece of furniture.

Joan sat on a red chair and looked at Ursula, who had shaky fingers from the speed she consumed all day.

"We have a parade today, and Honecker will be in it!" Ursula clapped her hands and smiled with excitement.

As her aunt handed her a cup of coffee, they watched the parade on the small black-and-white television on the kitchen table. Joan could only make out marching soldiers carrying a flag, and the horns blaring were mixed with static and sounded like baying dogs.

"I have a present for you," Joan said, trying to divert her aunt's hungry eyes from the screen. She pulled out the bottle opener and necklace and handed them to Ursula.

Ursula palmed the pendant and stroked the horns of the ram. "It looks like it could break anything," she said.

"Like the wall," said Joan. "You could break through the wall and live with Katharina."

Ursula's eyebrows lifted. "Now why would I do that?"

Joan handed her the bottle opener. "So you would have all the bottle openers you wanted."

Ursula gave a sad smile. "Oh, no, it's not important."

Joan gazed at her aunt, who returned to gazing at the television. Joan thought of her Jewish uncle who had died ten years ago, whom the communists had saved from Auschwitz. He had become a documentary film maker for East Germany, and they had raised their daughter, Katharina, in the East, their daughter who ended up in an insane asylum where she was made to paint the East German flag again and again with its compass and hammer and ring of rye and the black, red, and gold stripes. Now Katharina was alone in the West, separated from her mother by a colorful wall, barbed wire, trenches, and the death strip.

When Joan left, the sky was black and starless, and Joan felt heavy-hearted. That day it seemed that the wall would be there forever, separating families. In the station on the way back, the same old man, wearing green baggy pants and a black cap with a feather, asked her for a cigarette again. Joan gave him three more.

The next day she noticed on the wall, next to an image of a red bird, *Doubt is the Substance of Nothing*. She decided to get a bottle of blue paint and write underneath it, *Doubt is the Substance of Everything.*

Perhaps her aunt found solace in her orderly, sparse world. Maybe that gray stone was a comfort to her, unblemished by the chaotic color of graffiti.

One night Joan dreamed there were two moons in the sky. One was dripping red paint into the black night, the other glowing white, two craters for eyes. She wondered what the moon saw, whether it could turn and look at the other one, or whether it just looked down at the world with all its deserts and borders, its people collecting the tears of the red moon.

Joan's thoughts sometimes wandered toward Berlin whenever she saw Kate outside inspecting neighbors' progress of shoveling or weeding, with her short blond hair and frowns. Joan thinks of the corruption of money, control, and wants to fly back to Europe like her mother did, return to a city where you learn to live in concrete beehives, where you choose what borders to cross, and you bring presents instead of more rules, and if they take them away at the border, you always know you have more to give at home.

Joan Gets Her Funk
In Puerto Vallarta

Joan tried to concentrate on the task at hand. She needed to find a way to convince Natalie Williams, a nice girl, really, whom she knew from buying cigarettes at the 7-11, where Natalie worked, that "President Trump is gonna make America great again" was not really a very effective thesis statement. Try as she might, her heart was not in it. She knew she should be telling Natalie, "Hon, ya gotta be more specific," but all Joan could think of was white sandy beaches, fresh towels that she had not run through her own crappy washer and dryer, and cold, mind-numbing margaritas.

It was late March, spring break, and Joan had made the mistake of assigning an essay right before vacation. She, Jeremy, and Michele would fly to Puerto Vallarta while Darren worked in Nederland building a shed. Joan looked forward to it. In February she finally was off probation, and since then she drank moderately.

Getting off probation was uneventful. She knew the date by heart, February 7th, but on that day she received no notice and called in to get tested just in case. Finally, she called the probation office to ask if the probation was over, and they affirmed it was. Joan felt free, alive and now unshackled of the demands of her punishment.

Joan gave up on her final grading and went to the store to get an emergency supply of chocolate milk, remembering what her son said: "Mom, coach says I have to drink chocolate milk fifteen minutes after my workout or its only 40% as effective." She opened one of them and drank it, fantasizing about her upcoming vacation. She lived for trips to the ocean. She would drink tequila, go on snorkeling tours, eat fresh fish, and bury her body in the embrace of the ocean. She also promised

Alyssa a trip to LA in the summer, and she was considering going to San Francisco in May for the Alcatraz swim. Darren told her it was too much flying, but flights to California from Denver were short and cheap, and she deserved to travel with her newfound freedom.

Even in the plane, where her children ordered a huge bag of gummy bears and quarreled about who really should have sat on the window seat instead of "Mom," she was happy. She hated flying, so when she flew, she swallowed Valium. She was high. She looked at the bobcat on the wing of the plane and said, "Good riddance, Colorado," and she ate as many gummy bears as she wanted, because dammit, she paid for them.

When they arrived, she was surprised how large the city was. The streets were packed with people trundling along the crooked sidewalks with their colorful backpacks, scrappy yellow dogs, and burnt shoulders. As they drove on the bumpy cobblestoned streets, Joan felt a moment of regret that they hadn't chosen a smaller out-of-the-way town. But they would still have the beach and the tours.

The condo was spectacular. It had lovely green couches, terracotta-tiled floors, three bedrooms, and a deck with a view of the ocean. The beaches were packed with Mexicans and tourists, red and yellow umbrellas above tables from restaurants that lined the beach, children throwing colorful plastic balls, tourists strapped in skimpy bikinis sporting their burns. Jeremy looked at the crowds and frowned. He found the wifi password and delved into his phone while she and Michele sauntered to the beach and found a table. Joan ordered a margarita, took a plunge into the water, and strolled along the shore, dodging people who careened into her like those pesky jackfish when you snorkel. She wondered if she'd see any jackfish.

That evening, her feet and ankles looked burned. Joan bought some aloe vera lotion. The burn darkened, and that night she didn't sleep well, her feet and ankles hot and painful. The next morning the color was a deep reddish-purple, and spots were traveling up her legs. The spots were dark red, and they crawled up to her knees.

While drinking coffee that morning, she asked her children what she should do.

Because Joan's existence on the planet was for the most part offensive to Michele, Michele reacted by saying, "Gross, Mom! I don't want to look at your feet!"

Jeremy rubbed the blond sprouts on his chin. "Maybe you should go to the doctor."

Joan ended up in a hospital with stark white walls and a black floor that drank the morning light. The doctor was a handsome young man with short black hair and silver wire-rimmed glasses, and he looked as perplexed as her son.

"Has this happened to you before?" he asked. "Do you have some kind of allergy? It could be the sun. Hmm, it's spreading."

While normally young handsome men with accents made Joan want to have sex with them, she was too worried and scared at the moment. She was convinced she had the flesh-eating bacteria that either killed you or left you an amputee. Her uncle had almost died from that horrible bacteria, and once a neighbor of hers had lost an arm.

"Could it be flesh-eating bacteria?" she asked, palms sweating.

The doctor frowned and stared at the rash. "No…." He paused and Joan held her breath. "I don't think so. I think it's a burn."

"But it's purple! Burns aren't purple!" Joan found herself yelling, a habit of hers when excited or panicked, and she corrected herself and said quietly, "Well, the sun is strong here."

She stared at the black tiled floor and sulked. She wanted to have more time to sulk, but the doctor stood up and shook her hand, and a pregnant nurse led her out the door after she paid for antibiotics and antihistamines and the doctor's orders to stay out of the sun and water.

This meant that the next day, when they would visit the Marieta Islands, she wouldn't be able to snorkel. They would stop at a beach, however, so Joan could walk along the shore with her socks and shoes and watch the frigates with their thin black wings while Jeremy and Michele swam and gazed at fish.

The boat left early in the morning, and the water was rough. She and Michele got seasick. Michele visited the bathroom once, hurled, and then seemed fine. When Jeremy spotted a whale in the distance, he jumped into the water to swim toward it, which led to the tour guides yelling at her to keep her children under control. "Your child are the diablo!" one yelled. The tour guides were enthusiastic with the other tourists. They told a large man with a spandex blue swimming suit, "You are the man!" They sang and jiggled their hips. One of them had hair dyed blond, and he brought drinks to the Mexican girl, who lowered her eyes demurely at them and chugged the margaritas. Music from the 1970s and 80s blasted so the tourists had to yell at each other to converse, which they did. "Celebrate, Good Times" played by Kool and the Gang, and they asked Joan to "Come on!" She wanted to come on, but she had no idea where to go, the waves inscrutable ripples, her stomach churning.

When they reached the islands, the children snorkeled briefly but the water was cold, and Michele came back on the boat and said she hadn't seen much. Jeremy swam far away from the guides and one of them had to chase after him again, and then they yelled at her again. Joan sat in the rocking boat, visited the restroom to hurl, and listened to songs about getting your funk, the whole time thinking about the beach they would visit next and occasionally looking at her horrendous feet under her socks to see if they looked any better, which they didn't. In fact, they looked worse. The rash was starting to flake. She brushed off pieces of skin and underneath was a deeper red. The skin stuck to her gray socks. Okay, she thought to herself, I'm dying.

Finally, the tourists came back on the boat dripping water and ready to drink more, and they headed to the island with a beach. Joan couldn't wait. She would be able to walk on the soft sand with her socks protecting her from the sun. She would be able to enjoy the vastness of the ocean without throwing up all the time. She would see the universe's ripples and waves and beauty before she died.

When the boat stopped before the shore, and the guides informed them they would have to swim to the beach, Joan's heart sank. The boat rocked even more in the waves. She visited the toilet again and leaned over, trying not to inhale the stench of urine and shit. She vomited and watched the chunks of the breakfast burrito in the scratched plastic basin. She wondered how she could still be throwing up the same breakfast. It seemed like the vomit was bigger than her meal had been. She returned to the deck and sat another two hours on the uncomfortable white plastic bench, listening to music about partying and sex and having that endless funk in your life, and held her stomach. She looked up and saw frigates flying and a few clouds drifting in the blue skies. She watched the swallows dive into the caves of the island and envied them. She thought about the documentary she had seen about swallows, and how they were perfect mothers. Jeremy climbed the rocks to visit one of the caves, which the guides had explicitly said not to do, and so they yelled at her again. Michele played volleyball. She gave a skinny toddler the high-five and laughed.

Joan thought about her funeral. It would be a memorial, actually, because she would be cremated, and it would be in a room made of wood with a stone fireplace, like the lodge where she got married. Darren would feel guilty for ignoring her when she was pregnant, even though she had been fat. The dean of the college would bring roses to the memorial and weep with regret for paying her so little as an adjunct. Her sister Angelika, whom she hadn't spoken with in years, would remember fondly how Joan had taught her to smoke cigarettes on the shores of Lake Michigan, and all her past boyfriends would lament playing footsie with her best friend in front of her or making her eat asparagus just because their grandmother cooked it for them. It would be a crowded memorial. She started planning the places to ask her family to strew her ashes. She felt a little guilty. They would have to travel a lot—to Bali, to Berlin, to Vienna, to Columbia because she'd always wanted to see it and never had, and oh yes, to the 7-11 on

Belmont Avenue in Chicago, where she drank so many delicious coke slushies as a child.

The guides all had yellow snorkeling gear. They were nice to everyone, but when they looked at her, they frowned. She looked at her legs again, and the flakes were patterned like the waves, curved and parallel. When she brushed her hand down her legs, the flakes came off in little bits that stuck to her socks and turned them gray. Her children returned to the boat. Michele told her she'd won the game, and Jeremy said the caves were full of bird shit and not that interesting.

On the return, they blasted the music even louder. They served sugary, weak drinks you would have to drink a gallon of to get drunk, which is exactly what the tourists did. One woman, who offered Joan a Dramamine, was a 2nd grade teacher, a skinny blonde from Idaho who whooped and hollered when they played a country western song about how it was 5:00 somewhere, slugging her margarita, swinging her hips and snapping her fingers. Joan swallowed the chalky pill, then gagged and spit out the white powder. The woman asked, "Are you alright?" Her eyes were swimming, and Joan couldn't concentrate on them because the boat was rocking so much that she lost her balance and slammed into the Mexican girl. "Yeah, I'm great," she said.

Joan occasionally glanced at the guides, who were now entertaining everyone by wearing wigs and pretending to sing with fake microphones. The skinny one wore a long brown wig and a leopard-patterned shirt. Then she looked at the water, where she saw a humpback whale breach and slap the sea. She wanted to slap something, too.

When they returned, Joan felt better. She drank tequila while Jeremy watched a video on his phone about the latest school shooting, and Michele complained to her about the way Joan had sneezed.

Two days later, Joan's rash was almost gone. The skin had flaked away to reveal a fresh pink skin, bordered with white. When she showed her children the miracle, Jeremy shrugged and said, "Cool," and Michele rolled her eyes and said, "God, Mom! You are so annoying!"

They visited the village of St. Sebastian, where she looked at the image of the saint in the church whom the Romans could not kill no matter how much they tried, with sad dark eyes and swords piercing his body. He was wearing a white robe in all of the paintings, as white as Joan's new skin. Joan looked at his eyes. They were so huge. She wondered if her eyes had grown bigger through the years, whether as you approached death, your eyes grew. She opened them to the light. Eventually, they would cudgel St. Sebastian and he would die, but he managed to curtail death once.

Just like Joan.

Sharkfest

Joan had been thinking about triangles a lot lately so when she saw what looked like a shark fin, she panicked. Then she tried to tell herself it was her imagination. After all, that three-pointed geometric shape had been on her mind. Three as a number was dynamic and unstable. It's one of the reasons she had two children instead of one. Triangles were pointed like the head of a spear. Triangles were cruel. Her own family was a square that incessantly turned into a triangle where someone was left out, wading out in the miasmas of the universe as a single, lonely point.

Joan was all alone that May Day, yet surrounded by swimmers, lifting her head and struggling through the waves of the Pacific, staring out at the motoring freestyle of the others only to be plummeted by a wave. She choked on salt water. Someone slammed into her right arm. The swimmers passed her, their black wet suits like sealskins, hundreds of them, and then they were gone. The triangle, however, was still moving toward her, silver and shiny. Aiming right for her.

Why wasn't the shark trying to eat the others? Why was she always the sacrifice?

She'd torn herself in two giving birth. She'd given her milk to hungry mouths more than a decade ago but still felt it in her body. This swim was supposed to be about reclaiming her body and escaping the confines of her home, about balancing on a single point, the tip-top of a star in a constellation no one could read because no one understood her. A constellation that transcended the flesh. A constellation that was all hers. Now that beautiful universe pattern would be missing her body as she would be swallowed by a creature of the mysterious sea.

She'd decided to do the Alcatraz Sharkfest race the winter before. Everyone on her Masters swim team encouraged her to swim in open water in the summer, since she was mostly a sprinter and just swam in pools. But she hated Boulder's reservoir because it was filled with cow shit and e-coli and was so filthy, she couldn't see a thing. She would settle for nothing less than the ocean. She'd been swimming her whole life, so she didn't need to train. It was only one-and-a-half miles, which is about the same as the 2,500 yards she swam for workout.

Now she found herself pulled by the current and heading toward the Golden Gate Bridge with the triangle of the shark fin swimming toward her. She had also read that 1,800 people had committed suicide and plunged to their deaths from the bridge, and last year there were twenty-one confirmed suicides and four suspected, though no bodies were found. They were probably eaten by sharks. To top it off, the bay was filthy, no better than the reservoir. Also, the fog was so thick that she lost sight of the lead boat with its bright orange buoys to guide the swimmers. She started doing breaststroke so she could keep her head out of the water and see better, but she couldn't trust her eyes because of the fog and her preoccupation with triangles (was she hallucinating the shark fin?) She spun in the water and looked at the rippled waves disappearing in the fog. The shark fin was still heading for her, yet it didn't seem to get any closer.

She was reminded of how the moon had followed her as a child as she sat in the backseat of her mother's station wagon while being carted home from swim meets at night. How the moon, especially when full, seemed to drive alongside them in its heavenly place, a cosmic wheel on an otherwise invisible chariot.

She wanted someone to rescue her. She decided then and there that she was the most alone person you could ever know, and all the reaching out and connecting, all the triangles drawn in her square family so the square was full of lines like spears breaking hearts, all the talk and sex and general messiness of human interaction had been a waste of time because she was born alone, and she would die alone. A wave plummeted her and the salt water stung her eyes. She swallowed another mouthful and cried, her tears releasing the Pacific she'd just taken into her body back into the body in which she floated as once she'd floated inside the amniotic waters of her mother's womb, and it was absolutely true, she was both alone and part of the infinite wild.

Now her children were older and partying in their basement while Joan claimed her own power in the rough waters of the bay. Darren was at home starving himself and running ten miles a day, and she was about to be breakfast for a shark. Joan started crying so much that it was hard to breathe. She sobbed and deeply inhaled a mouthful of salt water, then coughed, her arms sculling to keep herself above water. A wave crashed into her and she ducked and coughed under water. She came up and took a breath, then hacked again. She heard a roaring sound, a harbinger of death, she thought, and suddenly a huge jet ski with a cop on it drove up to her and threw out a board and told her to get on.

The problem was, Joan hated cops. When she was in jail, the police were so mean to her. She was drunk and wanted to use the phone to call Darren, but they yelled at her and put her in a holding cell with a red mat on the floor. She couldn't sleep so she kept banging on the window and the cops sneered at her. When they finally put her into the jail cell, the policewoman, her mouth thin and tight, also wouldn't help her with the phone. She wanted to be rescued, but cops were awful people in an abhorrent criminal justice system and she'd be damned if she was going to get on that raft and be carried off by those abominable people.

Her coughing fit over, she turned to the policeman and said, "I'm okay. I can swim."

The cop yelled, "You're off course, I'll bring you back to the race so you can finish."

Joan looked around and couldn't see the shark fin anymore. The fog was milky and thick, and she was cold. She was freezing, in fact. It dawned on her that she had never been so cold in her life.

She grabbed the board and the cop led her back to the race. She found someone as slow as she was and followed him, and when she finally made it to the shore, she lay down in the cold sand, surrounded by people stumbling in their black wet suits. She shivered, her mouth tasting like salt, and decided then and there that all her assumptions were wrong. Cops weren't always bad, she was strong enough to conquer shark-infested waters, and no one was truly alone. You were only truly alone when you tried to be otherwise. You get what you want and need from others only if you don't expect it, only if you don't count on it. Life was a paradox.

When Joan returned to her Colorado home, the house was empty and unlocked. She cursed. No one but she locked the doors and they were just lucky they hadn't been robbed. She walked into the kitchen and began wiping crumbs off the counter and emptying the dishwasher. She sat at the kitchen table, took out a piece of paper, and drew triangles. She drew so many that they overlapped and became a fractal form. She took out crayons and colored in all the bordered spaces. She focused on red. She imagined that inside of her she was mostly red with all the blood and passion and general rose-like bloom of her spirit full of beauty and thorns.

Darren cooked them dinner that night, steak and scalloped potatoes, and asked her about the trip, then told her he planned on replacing all the windows on the first floor of the house. Upstairs already had new windows since after the fire. What she really wanted to hear from him was that she was brave. She wanted him to be impressed by her athletic performance.

He took a nibble of his salad. "These windows are old and leaky. We need to seal the heat inside for winter."

Joan cut her steak and watched the blood spill onto her plate. Darren always cooked steak too rare. "Speaking of sealing, you could start closing doors behind you and locking the doors."

Darren set down his fork and sighed. "Okay, Joan, whatever. Anyway, these windows are old. And look at the condensation here."

He pointed at the double-paned windows of the dining room. "We'll have clear windows to look out of."

Joan looked out the window. A beehive lived in their old willow tree, and she could see them swarming together through the window, basking in the summer heat. They would make honey and feed each other. Together they built a home. She thought how trust was as unstable as the number three and as solid as a trunk, even if it was hollowed out, even if there wasn't enough room for sap and root alone and it had to bring in the outside world. Nature was as crowded as cities, cities as fractal as love that knew no rules.

Joan thought how maybe they should live near the ocean, and she could learn how to sail, and she could see Alyssa more. She looked at Darren's handsome face, his almond eyes and chiseled nose. "How much will it cost?

"A lot," he said. "But it's a good investment."

Joan took a bite of the bloody meat and chewed. "Okay, I like the idea of a warmer house." She paused, cut another piece of steak but didn't eat it yet. Instead, she tried again. "Thanks," she said, "for the warmth."

Everything Comes in Threes

Joan had three wishes that inhabited her like rain clouds on an early summer day. The first was to have a career she could be proud of, the second was that her children grew up happy and healthy, and the third was to live until at least eighty despite all her addictions and self-destruction. She'd had three lovers in high school who left her: one went off to college, one couldn't deal with her crazy behavior after she swallowed a handful of sleeping pills, and one left her for another woman.

She had three addictions: alcohol, cigarettes, and sour gummy bears.

She had two children and always dreamed of being pregnant with a third.

She had three emotions toward her husband: love, irritation, and despair.

And today when she pulled a tarot card, she picked the three of swords—three swords piercing through a heart.

And now this day was the culmination of three falls from grace.

The first fall: She'd had an interview for a full-time teaching position that she failed miserably at. She decided to tell a story about a student and called him a "fuck-wad" because he always complained she wasn't clear enough about due dates. Then the gum she was chewing pulled out one of her crowns, so for the rest of the interview she had a crown rolling around in her mouth while she tried to answer questions about the college's program for student success.

The chair was wearing tortoise-shell glasses and a bright red blouse. "What can you do for student success?"

Joan said, "Well, you know, I see very little of that no matter what I do."

She was perhaps too candid. She didn't get the job.

Then her computer crashed. She hadn't backed it up for two years, so her entire most recent year of journal entries got gobbled by the black hole of her universe.

A week later, she went on a run and tripped over a willow root. She shredded her knee, and although they stitched some of it up, a giant hole remained, filled with pus.

The pus was the color she'd learned in her painting class to always use last. "Yellow doesn't get along with other colors," her teacher said at the time. "It's a rebel, unruly, a final touch."

So Joan had a complicated relationship with the color yellow.

When she was in college and had just traveled through Greece, eventually landing in Crete where she had eaten bread and olives, drunk in the sun and sea, and saved a starving yellow dog by feeding it her bags of biscuits and stale bread, which Joan devoured every evening dunked in wine. When the sun had set, she swam naked with tourists from Australia in the clear blue water of the sea under stars that had shined with the light she then felt, a subtle burning like her love for all the men who left her.

His yellow rain jacket glowed in the rain. She had come off a train to Salzburg, after spending the day talking to an Austrian woman who had a crippled mother and decided to see the whole world before her whole family died. Joan walked the cobblestoned streets in search of shelter. She wiped the rain from her face to keep it out of her eyes.

The man in the yellow jacket approached her. "Where are you going?" he asked.

The hostel," she replied.

The rain trickled down his yellow coat but slicked his brown hair against his handsome face.

"I know where that is," he said, "let's walk together." He pulled the hood over his face, his cheeks a round moon in the dark night.

He told her all about his studies as a graduate student in psychology. He talked about Freud, projection, and penis envy. The latter she didn't quite understand, because she thought penises were a bit wrinkly and pathetic looking, broken mufflers dangling from old cars, but she did like them when they were hard and inside her from a man she loved. And she had loved many men.

The man whom she loved at this point was a bisexual German blond. Before she left for this trip, they had sworn their fidelity to one another, partly because his boyfriend was in jail.

Now Joan walked through streets with the man in the yellow rain jacket, the cobbled stones and lights reflecting in the rain, and when they arrived, the hostel was already closed for the night.

"You can stay with me," he said. "I live close by."

Joan just wanted to sleep.

But it wasn't close. They walked along the river for an hour through torrential rain, and Joan was soaked, cold, and miserable. He talked to her about Jung's idea of individuation, and how the hero's journey reflected his life. He talked about Odysseus and how he slaughtered all of Penelope's suitors. The yellow-jacketed man had traveled to the Nile and caught fish. He had fought his enemy in soccer. He had returned to his girlfriend, who had auburn hair and a body like Venus de Milo.

"But we have troubles in our relationship," he said. "She does not support me."

Joan frowned, rain dripping down her face. "What do you mean support?"

"She won't do as I ask."

When they finally made it to his apartment, she shed herself of her soaked backpack and coat and covered herself with a blanket he gave her. He sliced an apple and gave her half of it, and she ate the sweet crunchy pieces. She was hungry, tired, and wet.

In the last month, she had been to three countries: Austria with its mountains and brown and white houses; Yugoslavia with its gardens and cheese bread; and Greece with its olives. She had traveled in trains and slept in caves in Crete with hippies from Australia to wake up covered in red dust. She just wanted to sleep.

His apartment was small with a linoleum-tiled floor and plastic orange chairs. It reminded Joan of her Aunt Ursula's apartment in East Berlin. She lay on the floor in her wet sleeping bag and tried to sleep, even though the fluorescent light was still piercing her eyes. He wouldn't turn them off. It ricocheted off his empty white walls. His room was as stark as winter. There was only one poster on the wall, of an Austrian pop artist with yellow pants.

When she was drifting into sleep, images of naked bodies in the sea and feelings of regret that she hadn't fixed the zipper on her backpack filled her mind, until she was suddenly confronted with his naked body above her and a knife at her throat.

"Open your legs," he said.

She thought of the choices she could make. There were three.

She could open her legs and be raped.

She could twist her body away and see if she could escape.

Or she could scream.

She thought of the apartments next to her, how her mother had always told her she had a big mouth, so she decided to scream. Her scream curdled through the room, carried beyond the walls like a hawk diving. She screamed from her hungry gut and her cold. She had never known what a voice she could have.

He jumped off her. She grabbed the knife. She made him stand against the wall, her hand shivering with the blade aimed at him, and she gathered her sleeping bag and clothes. She left in the pouring rain, her eyes tearing and wet from the rain, so she lost her contact lenses and couldn't see. Her backpack opened and some of her clothes, sponges from Greece, and her special fluoride toothpaste that had been prescribed to her by a dentist in the states before she left, tumbled to the wet cobbled stone. She ran and let them go. A taxi drove by and she hailed it. She made it to the train station.

There she lay shivering in her sleeping bag next to other tourists who had decided to sleep there on the cold gray concrete floor. Surrounded by other vagabonds, she wondered why she hadn't stayed there in the first place. The boy next to her snored, and the rhythm of his graveling voice didn't help her sleep. She couldn't stop shivering. The cold, dirty concrete floor penetrated her sleeping bag, then curled up and rested in her bones. Trains came and went, the rhythm of their wheels on the tracks an intermittent roar. After spending the night staring at the sign for croissants and coffee, she got on a train the next morning to Berlin, where she was living at the time.

Whenever she looks at the hole in her knee, she sees a scream. It's yellow. It looks like the three things that she loves about her life: her daughter's dark, long hair that falls like a waterfall; her husband's voice, which heals or wounds the torn surface of her dreams; and her desire to run as far as she can toward a home.

The swords in her heart were as blunt as the sun on this late summer day, and her children would never trust a man who thought he was a hero just because he caught fish on their little St. Vrain River in her Colorado home, and her husband would honor her, always had.

Odysseus's sailors had opened the bag of winds in the hero journey, but Aeolus, the master of winds, had given them all but the west wind, and Ithaca became a speck as they all got torn further into the sea, away from home. But Joan, she had the west wind in her pocket.

She would give birth to the third child despite the lost job, the words that blew away, the wounds that she carried in her body like smooth stones from a riverbank. That third child was as tenacious as the sound of the wind. That child was she.

Washing the Dog

Joan was stoned in bed one evening with Darren, trying to read *The Heart is a Lonely Hunter* and overwhelmed by the intensity of it. Her wound was bandaged and healing slowly, and June so far was an unusually cool start to summer, so she lay under their blue comforter.

"Darren, the deaf-mute character, Singer, thinks he has a friend, but the friend can't understand him. I don't think he even understands sign language," she said.

Darren got up to shave. "Yeah, Singer is all about projection. Everyone projects on him, and he projects on his friend."

"But it's so sad. He brought him Mickey Mouse films at the hospital." She pictured Mickey Mouse blowing a house down. No, that was the wolf in that three-little-pigs story. She contemplated whether she should stop eating pork because pigs were as smart as dogs and she loved dogs. That's when she decided she was too stoned to read, so she set the book on the bedside table and pulled the red blanket to her chin and stared at the ceiling, then looked at her husband.

Their house from the 70s had a sink in the bedroom. Their bedroom was the one space that still reflected the funky 70s vibe the house had before the fire and the remodel. They'd repainted the walls, the accent wall a squash blossom color that Joan had chosen, and got the windows replaced, but otherwise it was the same with a sink next to the dresser. The toilet and shower were in a cramped bathroom next to the sink. Because the sink was part of the bedroom, she and Darren were able to chat while shaving or brushing teeth.

Joan was in bed, her book now lying on her stomach. She watched

Darren shave. He nicked his chin and cursed. He dabbed the spot of blood on his face with toilet paper and said, "Filbert stinks."

Filbert was the only pet they now had from before the menagerie was adopted after the fire. He liked to roll in poop or dead prairie dogs, and that morning he'd found an especially large pile of bear shit. Filbert had been so happy rolling on his back in the pile of poop, full of apple chunks, which stuck to his fur. He was getting old and Joan had developed a habit of letting him do things she wouldn't have stood for while he was a puppy. She had let him roll and roll until his back was covered. She'd rubbed him off with a wet towel, but obviously it hadn't been enough.

"I was just thinking about dogs," Joan said. She'd heard somewhere that dogs were related to bears back in the genetic tree. He was rolling in his ancestor's shit. She thought about how symbolic it was. Don't we all just grovel in our ancestor's shit? And yet we need to move forward.

"We need to wash him," she said. She pulled the warm red cover off her and realized she was already naked and ready for bed, so she rose and rummaged in the closet for an old dress with a picture of a leopard on it and slipped it on.

Darren sighed. "Joan, really? It's bedtime."

Joan touched his cheek and kissed it, then went into the kids' bathroom, which was out in the hallway and had a bath, unlike theirs, which was only a shower. She tripped on a towel her children had left on the floor. She looked at the shower. The shower didn't have a detachable showerhead. She also had no dog shampoo, but she figured moisturizing Aussie shampoo would work fine, especially since it had a picture of a kangaroo. Then she went downstairs with the bottle and poured it with milk in a red bowl. She'd heard that milk helps with exfoliating and cleansing. When she returned to the room, Darren was looking despondent.

"Filbert could use a bath anyway," she encouraged him. "You can hold him and I'll shampoo."

"Why don't we wash him outside with the hose?"

"I think he'd like the warm water better. Let's use the bath."

Darren looked at her with his almond eyes. She thought how she liked almonds. Maybe she hadn't eaten enough dinner.

"Hold on," she said, and walked downstairs to eat almonds, but all they had were lime-flavored tortilla chips. She ate a handful. They were salty and unsatisfying. She opened the fridge and got out some ranch dressing, then dipped the chips into it and began eating, but she really wanted almonds. After rummaging through the fridge again, she brought out a bottle of milk and drank some. She heard Darren yelling at her upstairs.

"What?" she called.

"I thought we're washing Filbert!" Darren yelled.

She stuffed her mouth with the last chip and returned. Darren was frowning, dental floss hanging from his fingers. She took the floss from his hand and coaxed him and Filbert into the bathroom. Filbert hung his head, and Darren sighed. The slate tile floors were the color of the stone in the mountains, and Joan thought about the poor people who worked excavating stone and how it was like the character of Singer in her book, the deaf mute trying to excavate language.

She opened her eyes and the walls looked dirty and dingy. "Let's wash this dog."

But Filbert was not excited. He tucked his tail between his legs and licked her hand, and Joan thought how he was mute and how she talked too much, and how in a good universe, there would be more balance.

She looked at Darren and then fumbled, dropping Michele's special acne soap on the floor. "There should be more balance," she told him.

Darren looked at her blankly. Then a light came into his eyes. "Yeah, that's the problem with washing Filbert in the tub. It's hard to get into and it's slippery. Poor dog. Hard to get balance. We need to just hold him."

Joan thought about how slippery the world is, the way it slides out of control. "But we can do it. Can you get a towel?"

Darren went to the closet and brought two towels, and she leaned toward Filbert and patted the bottom of the tub. It was like he read her mind. He jumped in and licked her arm. Then her heart broke because he seemed to love her so much and soon he would suffer all because of her. All because she didn't like him rolling in his ancestor's shit.

She turned on the shower and it rained down on Filbert, his black and white fur soaking his back and leaving a part in the middle of gray skin, and he shook so that Joan had to close her eyes. She protected her injured knee with her one good knee and the other foot on the floor. All the droplets looked red. She opened her eyes and her face was soaked. She turned off the water when Filbert was wet enough and poured another handful of the shampoo in her hand while Darren held his butt and said, "He's being really good."

Filbert turned his face while Darren massaged his hind legs with soap. He licked Joan's arms, Darren's arm, and the side of the yellow tub. The shampoo felt soft and smooth on Joan's hands, milky foam on his back.

Then they had to rinse him.

They turned on the shower and Filbert lunged toward the side of the tub. He crashed into the glass door and it cracked. Joan tried to push him back but he slammed into the back tiles and then stopped and shook, and soapy water hit her eyes. Darren yelled, "Oh, shit!" Filbert barked and scratched Joan's arm with his sharp claws and lunged into her as he tried to escape. A trickle of blood ran down her elbow. He still wasn't rinsed, so Joan tried to push him back, but then he pummeled into her again and hit her chest, and she fell over. Darren grabbed his back legs and pulled him toward the rear of the tub. Filbert's claws slid on the slick floor as he desperately tried to find footing. Joan coughed and then pushed Filbert's chest away from the exit and pinned him. She turned off the shower.

"How the hell are we going to rinse him?" she asked Darren.

"I guess with buckets of water. I'll get a bucket."

Joan thought about buckets while Darren went downstairs to get one. Buckets were wonderful, how they had so many uses. She thought about poor Singer and how his sign language had more use than just being understood, just like their taking care of Filbert had more to it than he was capable of understanding. She turned on the bath spigot and rinsed her elbow while Filbert dropped his head and curled his tail between his legs.

Filbert looked at her, deep brown eyes pleading. He licked her hand, and she ran her fingers across his wet black fur. "You'll be okay," she said. Darren came back with the bucket, and they poured water on the dog. Milk drained into the tub, and Joan thought about all the milk she gave her children when there were no words. The white spot on Filbert's chest looked like a cloud. When they toweled him off, he shook and sprayed water all over the bathroom. It rained. She looked at the tiles, how they darkened with the water.

"I'm glad we got that over with," Darren said.

Joan pulled a wet strand of hair from her cheek and sighed. "It's never over," she said.

The High Peak

The only thing Joan looked forward to about dying was the drugs. She'd had Versed once when she had a lump removed from her breast, and she had felt so wonderful—relaxed, like floating on a warm sea, light. Morphine would be great, lots of it. She would travel to the underworld and see her dead mother. Now she had to settle for alcohol, the occasional Valium, and pot. They were fine, but the hospitals were hoarding the good stuff. Then there are the drug lords and dealers. Maybe she should meet up with some from Mexico. Maybe she should move to Mexico, where it was warmer than this cool, early summer Colorado day.

The only thing she liked about hiking was the descent. She had just trudged up the mountain and was now on the peak, high and buffeted, where the air was thin. She was eating peanuts and raisins, and glaciers in the distance looked like white eyes with no pupils. The light was so strong that she felt her pupils disappear, too. She squinted and turned toward her friend Stephanie, Joan's arms wrapped around her ribs and shivering, the sky cloudy, and said, "I think you should just dump him."

They had spoken the whole way up the wretched mountain about Stephanie's dismal relationship. Joan was mildly stoned from a marijuana gummy, and the trail full of people, dogs, rocks, and dust. Joan hated this hike up Mount Sanitas. It was steep and crowded. To climb it you had to take large steps up chunks of boulders and dodge all the runners and hikers sprinting and dogs shitting on the trail. She loved Stephanie but really missed Alyssa. Joan hated hearing about the endless abhorrent behavior of Stephanie's boyfriend: playing footsie with her sister at Thanksgiving, farting loudly in public, bathing infrequently so he smelled like rotten mushrooms.

Joan's relationship with Darren, on the other hand, was lately uncomplicated. It was based on minimalism—beautiful blue boxes where they had sections of time to talk about if the squash was done or if they should remind Jeremy to do his math homework. The night before Jeremy had stood in the kitchen snapping his fingers and listening to music on his phone. Then he left them with all his dirty dishes and Joan was annoyed because it was she, not Darren, who put them in the dishwasher. That was the kind of tension in their relationship. Boring first-world problems. At night they just passed out with exhaustion. Joan never talked to Stephanie about her relationship because Stephanie wouldn't relate.

Watching a cloud move with the wind and transform into a face, Joan pointed at it. Its large Roman nose stuck out at her. "Wow, that looks like my mother."

Stephanie glanced up and shrugged. "I said it wasn't working out and we should meet to talk."

Joan sighed. A magpie flew below them, a bruise of black and blue feathers. "Stephanie, don't meet him. Just dump him. You always meet him and make up for like, a day." She pulled a strand of hair off her face, and two joggers reached the peak and joined them on the rocky precipice, jogging in place. One woman wore a blue raincoat, and the man had a tight spandex black shirt on.

Joan hated them.

"Good that you're keeping that heart rate going," she said.

They glanced at her and laughed uncomfortably.

Joan looked at the view of Longs Peak covered in snow, its silver rock like an old wrinkled gray blanket, and said, "Let's go down."

Stephanie wanted to keep talking about her dismal relationship and Joan just wanted to talk about dying. Darren's masseuse had pancreatic cancer. Joan had a new mole on her hairline that she figured was malignant. It was on the left side of her face and a mottled brown color, and she knew that cancer on the left side of the face was common because of driving and getting sun on it. And then there was her dead mother.

Joan had recently released more of her mother's ashes, this time in the sink. That day was a Saturday, and she'd spent it reading a book about people dying and starving in India. She was excited about an ancestor ceremony. She would bring some of her mother's ashes and sprinkle them in the fire. She would burn her mother's body again, give her to the fire. The ceremony was being led by Crystal from her writer's group who always wore purple and read tarot cards daily. Joan kept the urn in the desk in her kitchen with a collection of deer bones and bills.

She opened the oak box and tried to pour a handful into the bag, when Midnight jumped on the table and knocked half the ashes on the floor. Joan swept up what she could, but there was a thin layer on the floor, so she had to mop it up. She sat at the kitchen table then and cried, and Spot walked into the kitchen and created dirty, wet pawprints on the floor. She never made it to the ceremony.

Now she worried that a piece of her mom's soul was at a wastewater collection system after traveling through pipes that eventually joined all the pipes from their toilet. In other words, her mother was mingling with shit.

She tried to comfort herself with the thought that her mother was also bonding with the Colorado River, which traveled to the Pacific, with surfers riding on waves that carried her spirit to the shore, where crabs moved her to the beach, where people in skimpy bathing suits played volleyball.

Joan and Stephanie then descended in silence, drinking their own thoughts. Joan had to step carefully where the trail was steep in order not to fall. Joan's knee was almost all the way healed, or at least the void had closed and it no longer oozed yellow pus, but it creaked now, arthritic and cranky. She had to step even more carefully than the previous times she'd done this hike, going down the steep trail even harder in ways it had ever been before the fall.

As they walked into the forest, Stephanie said, "He even said he wanted to have a baby with me."

Joan said, "Well, that's easy to do. Just fuck a lot."

Joan thought about babies. Had she wanted them? They had both been accidents, actually. Michele burrowed herself in her womb when Jeremy was only ten months old. Had her mom wanted her? No, she, too, was an accident when her mother got knocked up in Paris and then her father planned the shotgun wedding and moved her poor mother to the dreary and dejected Rust Belt. Did her neutered dog want babies? Do all the copulating animals in the mountains— the mountain lions, bears, moose, elk—want babies? Do exhausted pregnant mothers want babies or do they just not want to be pregnant anymore? Do fish dropping their eggs and sperm onto a river's floor want babies? Does having babies make us eternal, so that when we die we live on in our offspring, because they then spend hours in therapy trying to figure out how their parents screwed them up? While they try to patch up the wretched world their parents left them, and somehow attempt to pay the phone bills and have babies?

The trees drank the cold wind and Joan unzipped her jacket. It was June, so why so cool? She had a fleeting moment of thinking that global warming wasn't real, though she knew it was. The trail wound down further into the forest. Joan felt happy now that they were descending and she could look at the trees instead of focus on trying to breathe. In Colorado, much of the lodgepole pine was dead due to beetle kill. Joan imagined all the little beetles with their hard-shelled bodies on the rusty trunks, boring into the bark, decimating the forest. The foothills would have no trees left, just rotting stumps and the trunks of branches strewn all across the landscape like a barren field full of corpses after a battle. The beetles would carry disease and descend to Boulder, munch down the wood of houses, enter homes and eat up all the furniture, then crawl on peoples' skin at night when they slept and chew them up so that they woke up with sores. The sores would get infected and people would die of flesh-eating bacteria. It was just a matter of time. But here the forest was pristine. Joan watched a hawk fly on top of a tree and listened to its shrill cry. They stopped for a drink of water, and Stephanie retied her hiking boots. Joan thought how Mount Sanitas' trail was created for a sanitarium, where people had eaten vegetarian food, hiked, and soaked in salt baths. Now that they were descending, she could imagine how it was healing to be on this mountain. It was like a shot of whiskey, no, like five. Or like Versed. Okay, not that good, but close enough.

"I think it will work out," said Stephanie.

Joan pulled her hat down over her ears, covering her malignant mole. "Okay, sure. It will work out. In fact, it could be beautiful."

Clouds began to move in and a group of five runners yelled, "Passing on your left." Joan and Stephanie jumped off the trail and watched the runners race past them in a blaze of bright petroleum products for clothes, their fists bunched in front of them, their faces red. Joan thought of Darren then, how much he loved running. She felt the sting of a cold breeze and looked up at the sky, searching for her mother's face, but there were too many clouds to find any shapes in the ashen white and gray ceiling, closed now to any blue. Joan and Stephanie continued down the mountain, their backpacks lighter now that their water bottles were practically empty.

Then a breeze whipped Joan's body and she stumbled off the trail, the air suddenly tasted metallic, she felt the skin of her face burn, and it hailed. Joan tripped and fell on her uninjured knee and scraped her hand.

Stephanie leaned down. "Joan, are you okay?"

The hail stopped, and Joan examined her body. Her wrist ached a little, and her injured knee remained the same. She pulled up her pants and examined her other knee. It was red but there was no broken skin.

"I'm fine," she said.

They continued to descend, and when they reached the bottom, where the next group of hikers and trail runners congregated at the trail head, Joan thought how sometimes she ends a race when other people haven't even started—she has her babies, she pays her price in punishment, she gives what remains of her mother away—and she felt triumphant.

The Happy Station

"Turn over," Joan heard. A bucket of hot water poured over her and the woman slapped her buttocks as she lay on the massage table. Joan's neck ached, her right cheek smashed on the table. A towel slid from her eyes to reveal her gray dead skin on the mat and the concrete floors. Joan had been thinking about the state of the world: global warming, a scary president, the poor honeybees, and how to get her son to stop leaving his dirty socks on the kitchen counter. Visiting Alyssa was good for her. Alyssa had no anxiety. She moved through life with so much grace. But here Joan was shedding the dead of her body.

Joan turned over on her back, looking at the Korean woman, who wore black lace underwear and stood suspended, the scrubbing mitt in her hand posed to start again. Joan felt her raw baby skin burn against the mat as she lay back down. The woman had even scrubbed her butt crack, and it ached now. Joan lifted her head and pulled her wet hair out of her eyes. A tattooed woman with a lion on her shoulder next to her yelled, "Ow!" and Joan felt proud that she was silently enduring.

The woman smacked her arm and Joan set her head back on the mat. She closed her eyes while the woman put the towel back over them. Then the scrubbing continued, and Joan felt her breasts being smashed and rubbed like dishes with a Brillo pad, her toes raked, her ankles abraded, her stomach scruffed. Just when Joan thought the woman had finished with a body part, the area was revisited. At one point Joan felt the pressure of a hand on her forehead, followed by the woman scraping Joan's stomach with all her weight. Joan gritted her teeth and told herself that she was like a snake shedding its skin, like a hermit crab outgrowing its shell. Through her suffering she would discard and disburden her body, her life, of all that didn't serve her anymore.

Buckets of warm water rinsed her body again and again. Finally, her front and back were done, and Joan looked forward to the massage and facial. But instead, the woman smacked her and told her to lie on her side, and Joan was disheartened. After her underarms and ribs and inner thighs were thoroughly scrubbed and rinsed, she was slathered in oil, smooth and comforting. Then the woman took a handful of what felt like salt and rubbed it onto Joan's sensitive skin. At that point Joan thought she would cry. This was the pain of the cleansing of the earth. This was a revolution of her body and soul.

The woman lifted Joan's shoulders and told her to shower and come back. The showers were in the room adjacent, with the jacuzzies and saunas. The room had bare, concrete floors and three tubs, no windows. In one pool a pipe poured cold water and in another an old Korean woman closed her eyes and soaked. Joan walked on the wet concrete, rinsed, and returned. Her skin burned, and she climbed back on the mat with dread. Next she was massaged, with the woman climbing on the mat and gouging Joan's muscles with her elbows. She turned Joan over and smeared a freezing cucumber mask on Joan's face and occasionally covered her with hot wet towels.

When it was over, Joan walked to the open room, her skin smooth as a baby's, and sat in the steam room to warm up. She felt similar to how she'd felt after giving birth. Proud of her pain tolerance, a bit dizzy from the ordeal.

When Joan had decided to come to California, she decided this trip would not be about accumulating, like taking her dinosaur fossil, but about letting go. She was visiting Alyssa in LA. They swam in the ocean, drank wine with lunch, and booked a day at the Korean spa, The Happy Station. They ignored Alyssa's five children, who gazed at their phones, chewed gum, and stayed up late watching movies. On the day of the spa, Alyssa gave the oldest the car keys of one of their three cars and told her to go take the kids to the beach. She and Joan hopped in the quiet electric car and drove through clogged streets, talking about their menstrual cycles, wine, and the president.

Now Joan was heading to the salt cave where they would meet, passing women with breasts that exceeded any variety of species in nature— some dangling, some perky, some flat. She went to her locker and put on the yellow T-shirt and shorts they'd given her at the entrance and left the locker room to enter the hallway of the coed section, which contained doors to various saunas. The hallway had a yellow pyramid, plush maroon chairs, plants, a white bust of a woman with a yellow scarf on her head, giant crystals, a shelf of small ceramic pumpkins under a painting of deer jumping over what looked like yellow waves, and a huge piece of petrified wood next to a giant ball of salt.

Adjacent to the salt ball was the salt cave sauna, and Joan entered the space and sat on a bamboo mat next to a Korean man whose balls spilled out of his loose shorts. A T.V. blared *American Horror Story*, and instead of her plan to meditate, she found herself fretting about the Antichrist's devastation of the world through nuclear weapons that reduced the planet to a toxic wasteland. When Alyssa entered, the coven of witches seemed helpless, and Joan was beginning to feel dispirited.

She said, "Can we just go into the jade room again?"

They shuffled with their loose sandals to the jade room, its green color soothing to Joan. It had no T.V. but instead played 1970's music, and Joan listened to Elton John's "Rocket Man" while contemplating whether the coven of witches could just magically transport themselves to another planet. Three Korean women sat staring at the walls; a hippy with dreadlocks sat cross-legged, meditating. Alyssa was staring at her purple nails and frowning. She was probably wondering what to do about her pothead daughter, thought Joan, but Alyssa leaned over to her and whispered, "I just don't think purple is my color."

On the way home, the L.A. streets snarled with traffic, Joan contemplated how she could change the world. She was worried about so much: the nuclear arsenal of her country, global warming, the dying fish, sea birds eating plastic, and beetle kill in Colorado. She'd been regularly writing letters to the editor of their newspaper, arguing for anything from abstaining from euthanizing bears, to arguing about the way the criminal justice system oppressed minorities. The bears got into peoples' trash cans and made a big mess (it'd happened to them many times), but it was their fault (especially the time Joan threw away the rotting salmon after her trip to Wyoming). She told the editor (and the not-so-good people of Boulder) it was on the humans to do better. The bears were not at fault. She had recently attended a demonstration against the Boulder police force that pulled weapons on a poor black student who was picking up trash in front of his dorm as part of his work-study job at the university he attended. She really did want to change the world. Baby steps, she thought, like her baby skin. Start with a ritual, end with a revolution.

"We're like witches," she told Alyssa. Joan felt elated suddenly, pure and whole.

Alyssa honked at a stalling red car in front of her. "I know, right? But I'm getting better at controlling my temper. I learned to count to ten when my babies were crying all the time to keep myself from smacking them."

"No, I mean in a good way," Joan said. "We're the mothers of the future."

They were driving along the beach with people playing volleyball, surfing, and building sandcastles. A young boy wearing a bright blue rash guard flew a kite, a green dragon. Joan looked at the city of crawling cars and the crowds of people rollerblading, playing volleyball, or walking their dogs. She sighed. Did they even know that the apocalypse was coming, and they needed to change the world, or at least vote?

Joan's back felt raw against the car seat. She thought of how she was always trying to peel off layers to get to the raw center of things, and then just ended up regretting tearing out the fence, abandoning her shell like a hermit crab that thought it could find something better, a shell with a pattern of stars instead of the straight lines of bars, a universe full of comets instead of nuclear bombs. If she kept peeling, there would be nothing of her left. She sighed. She wasn't sure whether she was trying to change the world or change herself. It was a kind of magic, like a magician leading a woman into a coffin, then closing her in the tight space. He waves a wand over it as the music rises toward an orgasmic crescendo, opens the casket, and she has disappeared.

Starfish

An anchorman on the T.V. looked like a turtle, his head disappearing into his neck as he spoke. Alyssa lifted her head, took a sip of wine, then collapsed back on the couch. The anchorman said, "In California, the starfish have been dying, their legs disintegrated into goo. Global warming may be the cause!" Here they showed a shot of a starfish with white, gooey legs that looked like glue. Then she saw the anchorman again, with slick dark hair and a blue suit and that sad lack of a chin, and he said, "The virus thrives in warm waters. But a hopeful story! The starfish developed a genetic code to survive, and now the beaches are full of juvenile starfish. They say if only we weren't so complex, and we could change genetically to adapt to our heating planet, maybe we would survive." Joan listened to the rhythm resounding in the house. The five-year-old Seth was pounding his fists on the kitchen table to the rhythm of Queen. "We will rock you," Joan kept thinking to herself.

Joan thought about all the wine, bread, cheese, and chocolate she'd eaten the day before. Alyssa knew of a bakery with the best loaves in LA, she'd said—big round loaves of sourdough that Joan had consumed voraciously while drinking cabernet. She dunked the chunks of bread in the wine like she had learned from the hippies in Greece. If she stayed in the house, she knew she'd eat more bread and probably dive into the cheese puffs, too, and get even fatter. Alyssa was lying on the couch drinking a martini with her hand draped over her forehead like a diva from an old black-and-white movie. Jeremy and Michele were wringing out their wet suits on the front lawn.

Joan was feeling fat, so she decided to go visit the starfish. Alyssa said she'd lend her the minivan, while the kids ate hunks of bread with peanut butter. They were also devouring cheese puffs. Seth was still pounding the table. The middle-schooler, Josiah, drank milk, and the teenage girl, Cameron, pulled down the blue bikini bottom from riding up her butt and stared at the contents of the fridge.

Joan felt like crying. She was amazed at the synchronicity of the universe, how she'd planned to visit the starfish anyway due to her corpulence, and now the anchorman (who couldn't help it, really, that he had no chin) was telling her that there was a way out. The human race needed to evolve.

Joan walked past the palm tree swaying in the wind and entered the golden minivan. After typing in the address to visit Abalone Cove, she drove through the traffic of Redondo Beach until she hit the curved road that led to the cliffs. She parked at the trailhead and descended toward the beach on the dusty trail.

When she hit the sand, she stopped to look at the rippling waves of the Pacific. An old torn-up concrete building stood to the left of her. It had been a preschool once, and one remaining wall had frescoes of sand and sea, of fish, dolphins, and starfish. Now the children went to preschools on the city blocks, surrounded by traffic and concrete.

She stood and looked at the frescos of sea life and thought about visiting the Minoan ruins in Crete, also with walls of porpoises and fish. The Minoans had been matriarchal. Joan instead had to visit church every Sunday growing up, take communion from an old priest wearing a white robe with glasses so thick his eyes swam. She ate wafers of bread from his hand and drank wine from a golden chalice.

The Christian story of the universe was really a trick that would turn on itself because that broken body would feed the children the women would carry in their bodies, then raise them. God was just jealous. Joan missed her mother. Sometimes she was willing to nail herself to the felled trees of the woods, where the moon reigned as it did in this ocean, tugging and pulling the water. There, her mother baked bread for her, loaves steaming on the dining room table beneath an oil painting of a still life of chalices full of wine.

She walked to the tide pools. The water was cold and lapped over her shoes. The coral was black and jagged, with pools full of crabs and mussels. She continued only a little way until she found a starfish. She bent down and touched its orange body. It didn't move. A six-pointed star, it contained a third eye, a heart, shoulders heavy with the world, and two legs that carried her nowhere. It was a star that fell from the sky.

Joan wanted another chance at life.

The Landing Strip

Joan returned from LA feeling healed and rejuvenated, but it didn't last long. It was September, summer had come to a close, and Joan was teaching again, Darren was at the tail end of his intensive work season and often cranky, the kids were on the verge of going to college, and Joan was dying all the time from mysterious illnesses. People told her she was a hypochondriac, but she knew, from watching her mother, that getting old was tragic. Her old dog Filbert was also dying, sleeping all the time and his hips atrophied, so she decided she would take up skydiving.

Heaven seemed so far away, unattainable even in her dreams. The night before she dreamed that she was writing on the walls of a metro station in Berlin, and she was late to see a doctor. She ended up in an elevator that kept descending, and a dark-haired woman gave her a piece of paper to write on, and she found herself scribbling, unable to produce a legible word. The pressure of the descent hurt her ears.

She needed to ascend where the air was thin and the sky open and empty—God's sleepy mouth yawning because there was nothing left to do when heaven was so perfect. Jesus rising from the earthen home that betrayed him, the way life had betrayed Joan. She was meant to be a queen but cursed into the role of pauper. She commanded her family and they saw it as begging, her words a mere hat of a busker where her audience threw pennies. She asked them to clean the basement and they didn't. She told Darren to cut his hair and he didn't, his black curls falling into his eyes. No one listened to her. And she was royal blood. Everyone was, she thought to herself. We are all divine.

Now she needed to spend her savings on a vet for Spot, her beloved, skittish cat. He was shitting tiny white worms. Joan bagged a sample from the litter box. When she took Spot and his feces to the office, the vet, with a red beard and wire-rimmed glasses, told her it was from eating mice.

"We need him to eat the mice, though," she said.

"Okay, but this could happen again. In the meantime, give him these pills." He handed her the bottle.

Joan loved pills. Once when Filbert was on trazodone for his anxiety during thunderstorms, Joan downed half the bottle with vodka martinis within the course of two weeks. She would sit on her couch in peace and not even do the dishes, her perfectionism drowned in sleepy bliss (Darren actually disagreed that she was a perfectionist. But that was just because he was an anorexic athlete and she couldn't compete with that. He also didn't understand the nuances of being a mother—the folding of laundry, the pureeing of spinach and sterilizing bottles for babies, the matching color of earrings and blouses—the wealth of details she needed to get just right.) She and Jeremy would talk about Nietzsche and the balance of the Apollonian with the Dionysian, and they acknowledged order while worshipping the god of wine and art. So what if she wasn't a perfectionist? The god of dance knew the blurry lines of the body. And when the bottle was empty, Filbert suffered during thunderstorms. While hiding in the bathtub, he would howl and keen, and Joan felt a little guilty. She tried to refill the bottle but the vet became suspicious and mentioned that there had not been many thunderstorms in the last two weeks, so she gave the dog Benadryl instead.

Now, in the tiny, sterile office adorned with pictures of heartworm and a poster for Science Diet, Joan leaned over and pet Spot where he lay scrunched and held down by the vet on the steel table wearing blue scrubs and wire-rimmed glasses. "Does it have any side effects, like sleepiness?" she asked hopefully.

The vet took a stethoscope and peered in the cat's ears. "No, it will just kill the worms." The doctor lifted his head and set down the stethoscope. His eyes darted toward the exit. He seemed bored with Joan. Handing her the bottle of medicine, he ushered her out the door. Spot yowled in his carrier the whole way home.

Joan walked into the house with the drugs, set the bottle in her cluttered pantry next to the pretzels, and released. He rubbed against her legs and swatted her. She sat at the kitchen table, turned on her computer, and researched charities she could support skydiving. She found the Blood for Life organization that provided bone marrow and blood donations to people in Africa with leukemia, and because her blood was pure and royal, because she was dying anyway and needed to crack open the ceiling of heaven, she decided she would raise funds skydiving to help the poor people steeped in poverty on another continent by giving them the blood they deserved.

She thought what Jesus would think now of the poor mortal people scrambling about on earth pushing out babies and digging holes in the mountains, driving on dusty roads in war zones, wiping their babies' asses, paying taxes. She could identify with the whole hopeless world; her veins were rivers of blood leading to the sea, and her bones were filled with the marrow of the divine that she shared with all human beings.

While she was hatching her skydiving plan, she was also changing the style of her pubic hair. On Tuesday evening, she went to a figure drawing class at CU, a Continuing Education course taught by an old hippy who wore long flowing kimonos and earrings that dangled and sparkled and touched her shoulders. One model, a thin woman with large, pendulous breasts, had a thin stripe of thick, black pubic hair ascending toward her belly button, the ends long, the rest of it shaved. Joan loved the look. She spent the class focusing so much on the details of the woman's crotch that the teacher said to add in details of the face and upper body, too, but Joan wanted to get the pussy just right and ignored her. She drew wavy lines of hair, smudged the charcoal, and continued with the details of individual hairs. In the end her drawing consisted of a rough sketch of a woman with a black thin nest of hair and a long tongue made up of strands dangling from it.

The next day, she looked up pubic hairstyles and found out that she had a postage stamp, a shaved small spot, and the lovely model had a landing strip: a strip leading to her pubis.

She walked upstairs and stood naked in front of the mirror in her bedroom and frowned at her pubic hairstyle. She had shaved it all the way down to her crotch, leaving only a red-brown circle. She would have to grow out part of it and shave the sides more. It would mean that she would have to go through an awkward stage of prickly hair growing toward her bellybutton, but it would be worth it.

On Thursday Joan had little to do. It was September and still green. Joan was teaching two composition classes on Mondays and Wednesdays with two students who reminded her of rabbits because of their large teeth, one who explained to Joan she had dyslexia, so she needed more time to write her papers, two young men who wore baseball caps backwards, one woman from Peru who couldn't speak or understand much English so Joan procured a tutor, a woman with a tattoo of Tinkerbelle on her arm, and the rest either earnest or bored. Joan had taught the class for the last twelve years so it didn't take long to prepare.

That day all she needed to do was print out the compare/contrast essay assignment, which took two minutes. She fed Spot medicine stuffed in a slice of hot dog and registered for the Blood for Life skydiving. She scheduled her skydive for three weeks later. Now she would need to get sponsors.

That evening at dinner, it stormed and the dog paced in the living room while she heated up leftover chorizo with peppers using the stovetop and a heavy cast iron skillet slick with hot olive oil. Darren came home covered in bright orange paint.

"Look at this color," he said while opening a beer and pointed to the splatter on his legs. "They decided to paint the door orange and it looks awful."

"Well, it's a perky color," said Joan.

A flash of lightning cracked and filled the kitchen with light. Thunder boomed. The birds sang. The rain poured from the sky. Filbert whined. Darren grunted. "Did you find more work yet?"

"No, but I'm going to skydive for charity."

Darren held the bottle of beer in suspension while he froze and stared at her, then took a slug. He wiped his mouth. "Shit, Joan, not again."

"What do you mean *again*?" Joan walked to the dog, who panted and slobbered on the rug, and petted his head. "Poor Filbert." She went to the pantry to get the Benadryl. She poured out a pill and stuffed it in the back of Filbert's mouth.

The thunder grumbled, and Darren said, "I mean how you always distract yourself with crazy ideas. Please just focus on finding more work. We need the money."

It was true that after the fire, they had burned through more money than the insurance had paid, and they were also stressed about paying for their now expensive children on the verge of college. But Joan thought about how lucky they were compared to many others. "Not as much as the poor people in Africa dying of leukemia," said Joan, clenching her fists, ready for a fight. Out the window a flash of lightning split across the sky over their willow tree, its heavy branches cowering to the ground. She wondered how it would feel to be hit by lightning, to feel the electricity soar through her body and create a latticework from her branching veins. Filbert scratched the walls, and she felt guilty for eating all his trazodone.

"Why don't you just help your family by helping pay the goddamn bills!" Darren yelled. Thunder joined him. Filbert barked, then howled plaintively.

"Fuck you!" Joan walked to the liquor cabinet, poured herself a shot of whisky, downed it in one gulp, and stomped to the stove. The chorizo was charred and crusty, but she took a bite, and its spicy, hot, burnt flavor was perfect with the whiskey, and it burned her tongue, flashed in her mouth, and she thought how surely the universe was giving her a message of how she would fall from the sky and set fire to her world. Then she thought about her asshole husband, standing next to her and complaining as usual, like a dirty dark stain that knew no passion for universal problems and didn't understand her sacrifice. "You're just so selfish!"

"Fuck you!" Darren yelled back.

As usual, they dropped it. The children came home soaking wet, Jeremy smelling like theater popcorn and Michele with a new hickey on her neck, this one shaped like a squirrel, a body under her ears and a tail reaching down toward her clavicle. It made Joan think of her landing strip pubic hairstyle she was working on and the streak of hair striking her clit. She drank another shot of whiskey and told Jeremy that his contacts would be in tomorrow and she would pick them up. She told Michele that her hickey was beautiful but she might want to cover it up better, and she had the perfect concealer for her that she bought at Walgreens. Darren told Jeremy that the president was a moron, Jeremy agreed, and Darren asked Michele about her math test, which Michele had aced.

That evening while in bed, Darren read the paper and commented on a special kind of worm in Africa that lived in your eyeballs and how the tweakers in Portland were taking over the city.

"Those are the people I'm trying to help, Darren, those poor people in Africa," she explained.

Darren set the newspaper down on his lap. "Joan, skydiving is for wussies. There's no sport in it. Why don't you run a marathon or something?"

"I'll be flying! When have you flown?" Joan turned to him and decided she hated him.

"It's stupid, Joan. And you won't be flying. You'll be falling. There are better goals to have, like getting a fucking job."

"Fuck you," said Joan, and returned to her book.

"Fuck you, too," said Darren, and returned to his newspaper.

She tried to read a book with alligators in it while petting Filbert, who had recovered from the thunderstorm and was now farting peacefully.

Her tongue was raw and burnt and she worried it would get infected and never heal. Could a person get that flesh-eating bacteria in their mouth, she wondered before she decided you probably could because the mouth is wet and full of germs. She thought so much about her tongue that she hadn't paid attention to the two pages where the protagonist swam with the alligators and survived. Joan reread the pages and thought how skydiving would be like that—a brave act, a fall toward the sharp-toothed world from a sky so empty and big it could carry all the grief and dying, all the light it slashed at you like the tongue of God singing, cheering you on.

During the next two weeks, she emailed her friends, posted on Facebook, and went door to door in her neighborhood to get sponsors. Her neighbor was mopping her floor and hugged her and donated twenty bucks. Most people looked at her wearily and told her they'd already donated to PBS, the ACLU, or other agencies trying to instigate change. One neighbor, an old man who always wore a cowboy hat, told her Africa and blood donations were the last thing he was worried about, and ranted about the bear that ate his chickens. Kate frowned but gave her ten bucks. Some neighbors peeked out the window and didn't answer the door. In the end, she earned $130.00 for her daring, upcoming feat. It wasn't as much as she'd hoped, but she figured blood in Africa was probably inexpensive, so altogether it was a success.

The night before she skydived, she slept little. She worried less about the dive than the landing. Will the ground feel too hard? Will she break a leg? When she finally crawled out of bed, she dressed in comfortable black leggings and a shirt with a flying hawk under a cloud for good luck.

The field was still verdant, and the instructor was a young, dark man who instructed them to cross their arms, wait for a tap on the shoulder and then open arms, fly, bring arms to the chest as the parachute opens, and keep knees bent for the landing. She would be jumping tandem with a woman named Sasha who looked as young as Joan's children, sporting a shirt with Blood for Africa written on it in red. They would fly up to 10,000 feet and fall at 140 mph.

In the plane, they sat on benches facing each other, eleven people scrunched on the plane wearing red jumpsuits and a harness. The engine was so loud that no one spoke. Joan's heart beat fast, and she wished she had swallowed some Valium. She sat in the plane and realized she'd forgotten to give Spot his medicine that morning. She thought about alligators, her pubic hair, and her red toenails. Then she thought of nothing but her upcoming death while landing—bones shattering for the $130.00 to save some poor people in Africa. She would be a martyr for a good cause. There were worse ways to die, like rotting in a nursing home as her mother had done before she keeled over from a tooth infection, or falling off a building like her father, with no parachute to help you fall gently.

Finally, the jumps started. She watched the solo divers plunge out the plane's door first. When it was her turn, Sasha took her hand and led her to the opening. The roar of the wind was deafening. Joan looked out at the empty sky and square fields below her, littered with houses where people were arguing with spouses, sweeping cobwebs off corners, and paying bills. Sasha nodded to her. Joan jumped.

She fell through the sky but it wasn't like falling. It felt like floating. It reminded her of swimming, the air soft and gentle, the engine's roar turning into silence. It was nothing like a rollercoaster, which had always made her stomach rise to her throat. Joan was not falling. She was buoyant, sailing and drifting, hovering. She was like an angel, like a hawk, like a ghost. She shed herself of her body and became the sky. She was a cloud moving west with wind, tumbling through a god's mouth that knew no language, just the silence of the pause between breaths, the sink into a center blue and deep as sleep. Sasha spun her to the right, then the left, and deployed the parachute. Joan suddenly slowed down, and they dangled together toward the field for landing. As the green plains grew closer, Joan bent her legs, touched the ground gently, and began running with Sasha until the parachute fell to the ground.

Sasha smiled at her. "How was it?"

Joan was ecstatic. "Great," she beamed.

Joan came home transformed. Darren was installing trim in their kitchen, the nail gun freaking out Filbert, who barked ferociously at the noise. She wondered if he'd ever finish the remodel the fire initiated. After all, it had been more than two years since that awful day in April. Jeremy was scrolling on his phone on the living room couch, and Michele was nowhere to be found. Joan didn't even care about the noise. The silence of the heavens had calmed her. The adrenaline of the jump had receded with her fall—not a fall from grace but into grace.

That night she dreamed of visiting Africa and being surrounded by children in a desert whom she fed bubble gum, and an old woman, her face lined with sorrow, told her that all the elephants were dying, and Joan realized that she was wearing earrings made of ivory, but when she touched her ears, they were gone. She woke up and thought about elephants, how maybe she should do something to save them. They had rituals for the dead. They congregated in circles around their poached kin and mourned.

In the meantime, she needed to get up and find Spot, whom she couldn't find to bring in the night before. She got up and found him outside eating a blue jay on their deck. Joan picked him up, brought him inside, and jammed a pill in his mouth stuffed in cheese.

Two weeks later, Joan still hadn't tried to find more work. Her students were analyzing websites or writing about their gender identities. Her landing strip pubic hairstyle was looking beautiful, and the model in her drawing class was new, an older woman with a huge bush a lover would just get lost in. It looked like a squirrel's nest, which made Joan think of her daughter's hickey, so Joan decided not to get so representational and drew a squirrel sitting on top of the woman's pubis eating a walnut. When the teacher, wearing a kimono with peacocks on it, asked Joan what it was, Joan told her a squirrel foraging for nuts. She pointed out that the bellybutton was the nut. It was the place from which all our hungers began and ended.

Joan was aiming for the ground of her being, for the earth full of creatures that yearned. She was aiming for a game where she would win. She was setting the Queen of Hearts down so she could sit on a throne in a shrine holding a chalice of blood from which all the mourners drank. She was a beetle pushing dung up the mountains. She was an elephant nursing the future. Joan was anything and everything she could be. She was pointing the way to a country that had no name, no borders, no language, no seasons, no country, no tickets to Vegas because it was all a gamble everywhere.

She was Queen of the Empty Skies. Her tongue had healed. She would give up, let be, bask in stillness. Her pussy had a perfect landing strip with a curl of red hair covering where her precious clit claimed her magic. She would not die because resurrection was how life spiraled, spinning in the air and landing just right, landing perfectly.

As Joan Approaches Infinity

The skydiving became like a dream, and winter buried what little hope Joan had. Joan spent February crying. She was still underemployed. Darren was happy because work was slow, and he took up weightlifting and ran ten miles a day.

The day Joan couldn't stop crying was the day she decided she would join a bowling league. It started on a walk on the plains with Filbert in a fog bank so thick and on snow so crunchy with ice that no one but she was on the trail. She couldn't see the mountains, let alone more than a few feet ahead of her. There had been an advisory for people with sensitivities to stay indoors because the air quality was bad due to temperature inversion. The fog was tinged brown with pollution.

Joan walked the loop of Boulder Valley Ranch thinking the whole time about the wretched day still ahead of her and how she wanted to get it over with. She would teach her composition class, buy shampoo at the drugstore, and grade papers, essentially how she lived every day, and she realized that at some point she'll find herself in a bed, dying, and she'll regret that she only lived her life for its end.

So that's what triggered the crying, and the chanting session from the evening before. She sometimes visited the group of New Age women on Wednesday nights and they chanted together, mostly Tibetan chants but some from other cultures. When they sang the Hebrew for "I am," she saw an image like a Japanese print of a boy on a mountain peak from a postcard she owned, and he was sitting in the middle of the jagged peak. She came home and told Darren that she was sick of being stuck in the middle of everything: always the one to call her in-laws, pay bills, cook meals. She wasn't fat and she wasn't thin. Her hair was becoming a combination of red and gray. She worked and made no income. Everything she did was mediocre.

She told Darren that evening, "I'm like a little Japanese boy in the middle of a mountain."

Darren sighed and said, "You look pretty Anglo to me."

As she trudged through the sludgy snow and blew her nose, Joan thought: This must be a midlife crisis. She was about to lose her children to the gloomy and odious world; she had no career to speak of; Darren was getting old, in chronic pain from his construction job; and she always missed her mother, who had been dead for over a year now. She had died in August and this was the second winter since then. She also missed her sister, Angelika, but more the sister from her childhood than the adult.

Angelika had always loved her bologne and pickle sandwiches. She had always liked having Joan help her apply blue eyeshadow to her eyelids, then they danced in her bedroom and Joan placed Angelika's stuffed animals in a line on the pillows of her bed, the biggest to the smallest, the horse to the mouse. They danced while trying to touch the ceiling, and Angelika couldn't reach it, so Joan put her on her back and they both touched the ceiling. Angelika yelled, "I'm so high!" and they laughed.

She plodded along in the brown cloud. Bunches of yucca pierced the snow and Filbert chased a prairie dog. He disappeared into the fog. Her poor old fat dog. He was eleven and would soon die. Joan burst into tears again, rivers falling onto her cold cheeks. They reached a small pond devoid of ducks, and she thought of the poor fish with a ceiling of ice. How claustrophobic that was. She too lived under a ceiling of ice. Heaven was a cold, cold place that hoarded its dead and when was the last time she had even dreamed of her mother? She remembered only that her mother had been lost in the dream, and Joan got lost trying to find her, and they were going to miss a plane to Mexico. She thought about when on earth she had every known joy, and a memory of bowling as a teenager came to her—the lanes, the music, the beer.

The next day she started researching bowling leagues near Boulder. She had been to the bowling alley before, Cowboys Strike Again, in Longmont with her kids when they were younger. It was next door to the gun shop. She'd won all the games, so she figured she was good. After contacting a couple of leagues, she joined Strike the Record, which had an opening. She lied and told them she'd bowled all the time as a child and that she had her own bowling ball. They told her to meet them the following Thursday.

She told Darren that evening her plans.

"How much does it cost?" he asked. He was sewing a button on his work pants while she drank a martini.

"Only thirteen bucks a week," she said.

Darren lifted his head, his mind chewing the way it always did when she spent money or was about to. "That's fifty-two a month, over five hundred a year. How about just going bowling every once in awhile with friends?"

"My friends don't bowl." Joan burst into tears. "I have no friends who bowl!"

Darren frowned, pulled up a thread, looped it to make a tiny knot, and cut it with scissors. "Sure, Joan, whatever." He stood up and patted her back. "If you want to bowl, bowl."

Joan decided to start drinking beer instead of vodka for the next few days to get into the spirit of things. She also bought a bowling ball, a small earth with blue and white swirls. She started doing push-ups to strengthen her arms. She practiced throwing Filbert toys into a basket to work on her hand-eye coordination and aim, and he would return them to her to play fetch. The fog cleared and she walked on the plains and saw a blue heron at the pond and felt elated, the color of her bowling ball, the bird a sign that the universe supported her choice. Also, the league was called Strike the Record, and she would be thrilled if she could strike her record, since it was pretty dismal with her DUIs and such, and made applying for jobs stressful. The league would be like a dream come true. Like a Japanese boy climbing up to the top of the peak, cracking open the ice to heaven. She was tired of being the Hermit all alone above the world. She needed to start over.

On a Thursday she pulled on her striped sweater and black, stretchy pants, dabbed some rouge on her face, and drove to The Cowboys Strike Again.

When she entered, the first thing she noticed was the bar, which had mirrors framed in gold reflecting bottles and bottles of booze, and she thought maybe she wouldn't have to switch to beer after all. She met the group in lane five. A burly man, balding, with wisps of blond hair, introduced himself as Bob, and Joan made a note to herself that she would remember his name by thinking of Bob the Builder from the show her son used to watch. The second was a tall skinny guy with straggly brown hair, Forest. He was so skinny that she imagined long, thin trees. She later found out he worked in a kitchen of a café and loved to read comics. The third on her team was a transwoman named Harina who had a beautiful black blouse on and a string of pearls. Her skirt was a funky tie-dye that didn't quite match with the rest of her outfit. She had auburn hair like Angelika had, and the same slope to her nose, a curve as delicate and perfect as a crescent moon.

They stood next to the bar on the dark carpet patterned with green swirls.

"Why are you named flour?" Joan asked Harina.

"Harina means deer in India and the deer is my totem animal." Harina gave her a warm smile.

"Oh, I just know *harina* means flour in Spanish. I thought maybe your parents were bakers or something."

Joan looked at Harina's face and did see a gentle deer there, but she needed a way to remember the name. She imagined Harina as a person made of dough and covered in flour.

Joan noticed they were all drinking something different—Harina wine, Forest a whiskey and coke, and Bob beer. She went to the bar and ordered a whiskey sour, and when she returned, they began to play. Joan rolled a strike on the first try. She was elated. By the end of the game, she had lost, but only by five points. Forest gave her a high-five and told her, "You're in, girl," Bob gave her a lecture about planting one foot and sliding the other back "like scissors," and Harina and she talked astrology. Harina was a Pisces like Angelika, and this confused her with her deer imagery so she thought about her sister and how deer are like fish, always flitting away, always distracted.

In the following weeks Joan improved, and she was elated that she finally found something she was good at. The day of the tournament was a sunny April day, two years after the fire, and she walked around the loop of open space and drank the spring warmth, gave Filbert slices of turkey as treats, smiled at everyone she passed, and decided her life was an ascent into golden summers and lakes of joy. This spring would be the season of rebirth it was meant to be. This April the house would not catch fire and Joan's mother would not die—no one would because all the energy was concentrated on resurrection instead.

That evening, under the lights, she stood tall and proud before the lane with Harina cheering her on, Bob reminding her of her legs, and Forest picking nervously at his nicotine-stained hands. The team they were playing was called Don't Give a Split and consisted of all men. As far as Joan could tell, they really didn't give a shit, especially when it came to their attire, all wearing worn-out looking T-shirts with rock stars like Meatloaf on them.

Joan decided she was the goddess, the representation of the feminine with Harina at her side sliding with her rolls, curling her body, swimming into the waves, her womb full of bowling pins she would knock down to birth their future.

Joad did it. She knocked them down again and again. During the whole game, she only rolled one split, and though Bob scored the final winning strike, Joan did as well as any of them. Harina scored two strikes herself.

Afterward, she and Harina stayed up the latest, drinking whiskey at the bar. They talked about turtles, Detroit, and drugs.

Harina was wearing a green, sparkly dress and golden hoops for earrings. Her curly dark hair made Joan think of Angelika again, who lived in South Carolina, voted Republican, and collected cats. She was seven years younger than Joan. Now Angelika didn't talk to her anymore because Joan called her a cunt for never visiting their mother in the nursing home, voting for Trump, and protesting against abortion. She regretted it and missed her baby sister. The relationship had been her first experience in mothering. The lights were dim, and the mirrors behind the bar doubled all the liquor on the shelves. Harina looked like a goddess to Joan, with a long blue skirt and sparkles on a pink shirt.

"Oxycontin is what put me into rehab," Harina said.

"Doesn't it mostly just make you sleepy? Never was my drug. Makes me too constipated. Thai Stick is good," Joan said.

Harina rummaged in her purse, took out lipstick, and painted her lips a bright red. Bob came over and slapped Joan on the back. "What are you girls talking about?"

"Drugs," said Joan.

Bob's face was flushed. He swiped his hand over his balding head. "I'll just stick with beer, thank you. You gals did great, by the way." He sniffed. "Need to get home to the wife."

Harina waved goodbye and turned to Joan. "Once I was shooting up heroin with a homeless woman and two cops came by. She kicked one in the shins and they took her to jail. I got lucky. They left me alone."

Joan had an image of her cellmates when she'd been in jail, many of them homeless. "You're lucky. Jail sucks. No one helps you figure out how to use the phone and the food is really awful. I ate beans there that were in a puddle of rancid tasting water."

Harina laughed. "I hate beans. When my friend got out, they got her clean. Then she ended up on the streets again and last I saw her she was busking as a contortionist on Pearl Street."

"Cool. You know, you look like my sister." Joan touched Harina's cheek. "If we end up in jail together, I'll show you how to use the phones. But what I'd really like is to strike my record."

Harina smiled. "Amen."

Joan laughed and took a sip of her whiskey sour. Harina was like the deer that Joan once saw hiding her baby under a tree in the woods of the mountains, and Joan had made sure to keep Filbert away.

That evening in bed, Joan remembered taking nine-year-old Angelika to the fair in the parking lot of K Mart in Chicago. They spun around the Midwestern sky in the airplanes and crashed into each other down below in the bumper cars before they tried to throw pennies into bottles. Later that evening Joan returned to the fair with her boyfriend, Tom, and they scored some Thai Stick. Joan had never had opium before; it made the lights so brilliant despite the polluted sky and she'd needed to close her eyes and just stumble. Tom won a stuffed elephant, and Joan planned to give it to Angelika when she got home. When they climbed up the rollercoaster hill, Joan looked at the gibbous moon and told Tom she wanted to eat it—she smelled salt and butter—and Tom held her hand while they plunged down. Joan was terrified, the tracks rickety, and she so stoned she thought she would go insane like her father and end up carving leather belts and shellacking boxes in a mental hospital.

She feared failure, and yet she knew she was descending and she couldn't stop. What amazed her was that her grades didn't suffer like the other students'. Somehow she was fooling the world. The lights of the fair were constellations she couldn't read, and that night she had a nightmare that her crazy father was painting the walls of the hospital white. He turned to her in the dream and told her he was using her bones, which he'd pulverized and mixed with water to make the paint he was brushing onto the walls of their home. When Joan looked down, her legs were missing.

The next day she and Tom drove to Lincoln Park and smoked more of the Thai Stick. Tom lit the joint, and when he handed it to her, she sat back and thought about the day before, how it might not be a good idea, but then she did it anyway. She inhaled a huge hit. It was early fall, and the oak trees still had their leaves, curved like hands. They lay under their canopies and watched the leaves rustle in the breeze. They shared a bologna and pickle sandwich and talked about how much they hated math. Then the big leaves started reaching into the clouds. A crow descended onto the ground and rummaged in the leaves for bottle caps and crumbs. Tom said they needed to get back to school.

It was senior year, and Joan, much to her mother's dismay, had decided to just take one class after lunch—a gym class. When she returned to the school, the fluorescent light burned her eyes. Her gym teacher, an old woman who could have used a little exercise herself, led them through a series of dance moves, Joan in the first row with a mirror before her, and on her right was a girl with bowed legs. Joan saw everything as being on a black plane, and she had to work hard to stay on its surface, above it into the light. She swung her arms and stepped and kicked and balanced, while the girl beside her was falling through the plane, her legs buckling into the black. Joan was worried about the girl, that she would fall into the underworld, and she wanted the music to stop. She wanted to halt the whole world in its confounding tracks. She wanted to nest the girl in her bones, let her nurse the blood of her marrow. But she kept dancing, awkward and off-balance, skinny bones like a clumsy toddler scribbling.

After class, Joan popped a Black Beauty to rush the Thai Stick out of her system, her mind electric then. She did her math homework while watching *Gilligan's Island*, drawing graphs of what happens to X when Y approaches infinity, drawing its curve that had no end. She finished her homework and reviewed the problems. She felt a wave of pride that her mind knew how to approach infinity, that she could mother her sister, that she could knock everything down because that was what her family did, and then she could build it back up with the X of her chromosomes into Father God waving Y around like a trident.

She shut her textbook and notebook then, stacked them up on the coffee table, and nestled into the corner of the couch with the arm where the upholstery was more worn. She looked at the TV and clipped her toenails. She watched the professor solve all their problems, the Howls drink cocktails, and the movie star brush her hair.

Life was good on the island even though they wanted to be rescued. Maybe life on the island lost to the rest of the world was even better than if they had been saved.

The Circus

Joan covered her eyes and slouched on the couch. "Is it dead?" she asked Darren.

Darren was kneeling at the empty fireplace as if worshipping its lack of fire, as if supplicating to a home that he rebuilt after the fire. "Not quite," he said. "Keep your eyes closed."

Midnight had caught the rabbit from their backyard and was now passionately shaking it.

"Can you kill it?" Joan asked.

"Yeah, I'll break its neck."

"Why don't you drown it in the toilet?"

"Joan, this rabbit is big. Shit, two fucking cats. Cats don't belong in the suburbs."

Joan was under the blanket. She had been used to seeing carcasses, but she couldn't stomach the dying. She'd spoken to the corpse of her mother, white as a frostbitten toe. She'd cleaned dead squirrels and mutilated mice from floors using plastic bags to grab them; she'd dealt with gutted rabbits like this one before and the endless tally of birds, of red-breasted robins and blue jays as well, but the dying creatures— the still alive but only barely ones—she could not handle. Even Jesus Christ had quite a time of dealing with death, dangling on a cross with nails piercing him.

That night she checked on Michele and Jeremy as they watched videos on their computers. In Michele's room, she stroked Spot, who was asleep and curled on the foot of the bed at Michele's feet. When she returned to the bed, Darren was staring up at the wall, now mostly white but with some artwork they'd collected since the fire. She and her children always disagreed about what to hang on the walls because Joan preferred artwork of naked figures, Darren landscapes, and the kids wanted posters of rock stars.

"We should have eaten it," Darren said as she snuggled up to him. "It wouldn't have gone to waste. There would have been a reason."

Joan turned toward him and kissed his shoulder. "I do like rabbit," she said.

After a restless night sleeping, where Joan dreamed that it was raining and Darren grabbed her arm, panicked, and told her that he had not poured a new foundation, and that the house would fill with water and soot, Joan woke up with her heart racing. The furnace hummed, and she rose. Still under the red blanket, Darren was sleeping quietly, and Joan slid out of bed at 5:00 a.m., unable to sleep, and walked downstairs to drink coffee and read about the circus.

Joan had never been to a circus. The Butch Cassidy Circus was in a small town, Peak, an hour's drive away. She had tried to talk the family into going, but they were not interested. It was at noon that day. She made herself some eggs, fed the birds, and cuddled with her terrier mutt Dexter she had recently fostered on the couch. He was black and white, with wiry fur and short legs. Darren had said no more pets, but she'd assured him it was only a foster. However, she was getting attached. He pushed his nose into her arm as she drank coffee and she scratched his neck.

She drove to the circus late morning. The sun was already stronger, touched her eyes with more verve. Joan loved the spring. The circus was a small one, set up in a yellow and green field. It was April, the month everything in Colorado started to green. April always made Joan think of the fire, and today was similar to that day, cool and verdant. The white tent bulged round as a breast, and people stood in line to get in. A man with a brown hat festooned with feathers took tickets, and Joan handed him hers and smiled at him. He returned the smile, his teeth broken and yellow, and said, "Enjoy the show."

Joan sat on the wooden bench wishing there was a back to lean on. She bought a bag of peanuts from a young boy dressed in black and gold and ate them, wishing they had more salt. In front of her was a ring made up of white tape. Music blared out of speakers, a kind of bluegrass jig, if there was such a thing, and a young couple, their bodies muscled and lithe, walked to the center of the circle.

The man raised the woman above his head, the woman contorted her body into shapes—arms like stars, tumbling like jacks. The man did back handsprings and the woman performed aerial cartwheels. Then two more people came out and held a pole, and the woman and man jumped on it and did flips, landing perfectly on the pole, and Joan thought how wonderful it would be to be so graceful, to have such perfect aim with your feet.

Then the clowns came running out to the stage, one a midget, followed by a green Volkswagen Beetle. They danced and skipped, threw pies in each other's faces, and kicked and tumbled. Joan bought popcorn and considered writing the circus and letting them know the peanuts needed more salt and the popcorn less. It had been a little less than two years since her last food review had been published, a short piece about Terry's Tavern where she'd overly criticized the fried chicken because it didn't taste like the fried chicken you could buy in Chicago. It wasn't that it was terrible fried chicken and she'd said as much when she also said her 2 1/2 stars out of 5 were strictly based on emotions. She watched the clowns tie a rope on the car and try to move it. One pretended to drink something out of what looked like a big black box.

Finally, the tigers came, slinking in with a man holding a whip and wearing a black bodysuit. He made the tigers sit up, jump through hoops, fly over torches, and roll over. Their back legs looked atrophied.

When the elephant came out, Joan was already feeling depressed and questioning why she came. She bought a Coke and washed the salt out of her mouth. The elephant looked like it had scars on its back, and the trainer, who wore a patch over one eye and was dressed in shiny gold pants, made the poor elephant sit, jump over hoops, and offer her back to him as he rode her around the ring. The acrobat came out and did flips on its back, and Joan wondered how that must feel to it, the weight on its spine. Joan thought about all the weight she carried of the world, and she felt like crying. She choked on a popcorn kernel and coughed, then downed the entire Coke and briefly considered a cigarette.

After the show, Joan milled about outside of the tent. She smoked a cigarette and stared out at the field. The plains stretched toward a flat horizon peppered with ramshackle white homes. She wondered why on earth a small town on the plains would be named Peak, although she could see the mountains in the distance, small and craggy on the western horizon. People entered their cars and left, and the crowd thinned.

Joan thought about the poor elephant. She knew elephants were smart. They performed rituals for the dead. Joan choked up as she imagined herself as an elephant, mourning her parents' death, mourning her upcoming death. She saw Darren coming out of a burning house, his face blackened with soot. She saw herself walking across ashes to find a shelter for her family, saving animals like Noah when the rain comes, when the fire dies and the water rises. She looked up at the wide blue sky, its maw as big as God.

To resurrect. To save.

She had already taken on everyone's sins.

She was the key that turned the engine's motor, the clutch that determined the speed, the wild that broke through cages, twisting metal, wrenching nails from her cross to journey to heaven. She imagined the sun descending and swirling over her head, becoming a halo. It was the same sun that burned her house, that purged her of all she didn't need, stripped her bare and made her start over with nothing but her living progeny and her spirit. She imagined herself holding a golden key to heaven. It would be heavy, and she would be strong enough to carry it.

The circus crew was busy. The midget was picking up soda cans and discarded peanut bags. He'd taken off his red nose, but his face was still white, and now his fleshy pink nose in contrast made his face look like a pepperoni pizza. The acrobats were picking up animal shit in plastic bags, and one man who wasn't in the show stood on a ladder, his butt crack showing through his dingy jeans as he tied a loose rope on the tent. The tiger trainer was messing with the speaker, turning knobs.

The man with the feathers and broken teeth emerged from a tent, glanced over at her, and walked toward her after she had come outside to stand and smoke on a patch of dirt before the parking lot, which was also dirt. He had a subtle limp and a long beard, the feathered hat throwing a shadow over his face. "Do you have a cigarette?" he asked.

Joan handed him one and took out her lighter. "Loved the show," she lied. "What's the elephant's name?"

"Mary Jean," he said. "She came from Texas." He preened one of the feathers on his hat. His hands looked dry and rough.

Joan had never been one for small talk. Even as a teenager, she would change the subject if her friends were talking about something like the weather. She would say the clouds moved from the breath of gods, or when they seemed out of sorts, she would tell them that perhaps their uterus was wandering, and what they really needed was an orgasm. Joan took a hit of her cigarette and looked into the man's kind brown eyes. "Is she happy?" Joan asked. "Is she well taken care of?"

He kicked at a rock in the dirt and looked at the ground. She joined his gaze and watched a beetle trudge away from them, its black back covered in dust. She looked back up at his downcast, frowning face. She could see that he was thinking.

The next day was Sunday, and Joan rented a huge truck, bought the elephant peanuts and carrots, and filled the back of the vehicle with hay she stole from a barn a mile from her house from a family that kept horses but were never home because they worked so hard to afford them. She returned home and sat on her green couch and researched elephant training and found out that elephants were trained in German. Joan could speak German, and the synchronicity made her more certain than ever that the universe was leading her toward this moment. God was swallowing her, joining heaven and earth in her body that had already done so much—birthed two children out of the cleft of her, climbed the wretched stone peaks of Colorado, survived fires.

"Ich werde den Elefanten retten," Joan whispered to herself. *I will save the elephant.*

That evening she and Darren drank some whiskey in the kitchen. Darren was scrubbing rabbit blood off his shoes, the water in the sink a weak rusty color as it swirled down the drain.

"Joan, it was awful. I couldn't decide for a while whether to kill it. It was moving, but Midnight gashed its neck to the bone. I broke its neck and there wasn't a sound, just a feeling of snapping. I still don't know what you were thinking when you got these cats."

Joan thought about Mary Jean and how she would more than make up for the dead rabbit in the grand scheme of the universe, but she wouldn't tell Darren yet, because he would be outraged and remind her that she'd been to jail once, and it was true she hadn't liked it at all.

Their life was too chaotic, too many doors opening and closing, teenagers spilling in and out of the house, the dog door the cats had figured out, and now came in and out all the time.

Darren looked at Spot darting outside the glass doors, frowned, and shrugged.

Going to bed, Joan set her alarm for 2:30 a.m. and kissed Darren on the cheek. She opened the drawer next to her bed, took out the dinosaur fossil, gave it a kiss, put it away and crawled into bed. She fell asleep and dreamed she was climbing a Christmas tree in a forest, and Darren was going to cut it down and bring it home. She yelled down to him not to cut it while she was still climbing. She began to descend. Darren was on the forest floor, a dangling axe in his hand. She fleetingly thought of the ornament of the cow painted with stars with golden wings. She wondered whether they still had that ornament. At 2:30 a.m., her alarm woke both her and Darren up, and he asked groggily, "Why did the alarm go off?"

"I'm going to steal an elephant from the circus," Joan said softly.

Darren groaned. "Okay," he said, and rolled on his side and fell back asleep.

Joan liked driving in the dark. The stars were out, and the moon was waxing, almost full, just a sliver missing from its left side. After an hour, Joan arrived.

The tent was down and wrapped up, its white tarp looking like defeated sails, and huge trucks and trailers were parked on the yellow grass. She had texted Nat when she parked, and she saw him now as he sauntered toward her, hatless this time. Tents were strewn on a patch of grass where the crew slept, and the lights from the parking lot washed the field in a blue light.

She stood next to the truck and leaned against it. Nat approached her and said, "We have to be quiet."

They walked toward the large trailer in front of Joan's on the dirt driveway and Nat opened up the back. Joan looked at Mary Jean and wondered how they were going to back her out. She could see in the moonlight a thick chain tied to the side of the trailer. Mary Jean's head drooped, and her trunk curled sideways on the floor.

They hopped into the front and Nat opened the back and then came forward and unlocked the chains with giant iron keys. He threw a rope across Mary Jean's back and they backed her out easily. Joan had brought a ramp to get her inside her truck, but Mary Jean balked at the entrance and leaned back. Joan was in the back of the truck coaxing her and tugging at the rope, and Nat leaned his skinny body against the elephant's hip, the power of his weight nothing to her. Finally, Joan walked down the ramp to Mary Jean and stroked her. Her rough skin was full of tiny folds. Joan then pushed her from behind, but the elephant still wouldn't budge, not even with both of them pushing on her butt.

"Shit," said Joan, "how are we going to get her in?" Joan thought she'd try German. "Herein," she told Mary Jean, but the elephant didn't move.

Nat handed her the rope and jumped in the back and held out the carrot. "Come on, Mary Jean," he said, "you're going to a better home."

The elephant leaned back, the rope taut now, Joan beginning to lose her balance. In front of her was an elephant leaning on its haunches, strands of hay, and piles of shit.

Suddenly the woman acrobat appeared, dressed in a white T-shirt and leggings, and asked, "What's going on?"

Joan's heart sank. They were caught. She'd end up in jail. The mean policewoman with the butch haircut and fat ass would sneer at her again and refuse to teach her how to use the phone. Darren would be angry. Shit, lawyers were so expensive. She looked at the woman and thought about how the woman's body could bend and dance and push limits. So Joan tried a Hail Mary.

"Can you help?" she asked. "I promise I'll bring her to a better home."

The acrobat snapped her head back and forth, as if she were trying to find a way to escape. But she stood still and then looked at the elephant. Finally, she walked to Mary Jean's head and stroked her ears. She cooed and whispered something in her ear. She kissed the gray, leathery neck. Joan moved to the front, stroked the trunk, and then took hold of the rope and gently tugged it, her body halfway up the ramp. Mary Jean took a tentative step.

Joan jumped into the truck and said, "Ich werde dich nach Hause bringen." *I will bring you home.* Mary Jean lifted her trunk, and Joan looked into the black hole of it as the elephant brought the trunk back down, reached toward her. Mary Jean stepped toward her and walked up the ramp, and Joan thanked her. "Danke."

While Joan was driving, she smoked a cigarette and headed northeast toward the sanctuary Into the Wild. She'd been once before with Jeremy when he was a toddler. It was a contained wild like a National Park, a place where animals could roam and be safe—bears hibernating in dens, tigers swimming in pools, lions healed by veterinarians from their damaged paws after living in concrete cages. They hadn't seen an elephant there, but Joan knew they would take Mary Jean. She would make sure to escape after dropping her off. She liked the idea of being the invisible savior.

As she turned the truck into the dirt driveway, a pair of bright eyes flashed out of the dark. A fox stopped and stared at her, its eyes glowing in the headlights. She stopped the truck and watched it. Its sleek red form glowed fire. It was a ghost, Joan decided. Was it her mother? Dying had been so gruesome for her mother—the labored breathing, the sweating—that Joan had been relieved when it was finally over. She thought of the house fire, how it had been a kind of death, how now she was living as a ghost now and somehow she needed to make up for it by committing to the flesh, the material of life, the rebuilding, the body.

How she would dig the graves and let the eggs hatch. How she would give life a second chance. When she arrived, light illuminated the night on a porch of the white house in front of the sanctuary. Joan led Mary Jean out of the truck by coaxing her with carrots, then tied her to a tree. A winking red light flashed. She looked directly at it and her eyes were blinded by it. A camera? She walked to the door, air cool against her face, rang the bell, then bolted.

Speed Bumps

Two years later, burned out on Zoom classes but loving her pets more than anything, her court case for stealing Mary Jean had been dismissed because Joan had a kick-ass lawyer, who'd agreed to represent her pro bono because of the good she'd done, and Joan was protesting the changes in her community about the change of the 25 mph speed limit to 20 mph. Mary Jean lived in the sanctuary, and Joan visited her occasionally, watched her amble free on the plains, her trunk swinging like a metronome.

The pandemic had barely waned, despite vaccinations. She had allowed herself to be poked to save humankind, a sacrifice that had certainly had its cost. She'd had a fever and a swollen arm for days. But now she was healthy and her only project was to transfer an exorbitant amount of money to CU, where Jeremy and Michele were in college. Joan was suffering from the ennui that plagued her so often, now worse due to the pandemic. She was even mildly depressed, languishing. She was collecting coins she couldn't spend anywhere, giving the few she had to the liquor store which was out of them, and reading about bamboo, military airstrikes, and corneas. She was stepping in people's footprints when she took walks on the neighborhood trail. Rarely did she venture outside of the neighborhood, since the two classes she taught were through Zoom, and she'd fostered two aggressive dogs that tried to attack the other dogs off leash and when one, Cody, had jumped on a tiny, leashed poodle in the neighborhood, she gave them up. Darren had already said that Dexter, their new terrier, the cats, and the birds were enough.

Sometimes she thought of her mother and wept that she had not been there when she had died. Or she staked her shefelera plant to help it become tree-like, mourning its diminutive life. Or she cried in the basement when collecting the sticky strips that killed the spiders, lying next to her children's bong she had failed to get rid of, their desecrated bodies shriveling inwards. But mostly her life was an opening up.

But there was still a shutting, a closing, a kind of imprisonment that Joan couldn't shake. Boulder was constructing speed bumps everywhere, or strange sections blocked off to two-way traffic so that you had to swerve left and right or stop and pour exhaust into the air when a car came your way. She collected people to support her from Next Door.

Her children were gone. Sometimes she looked at them when they visited from across the dinner table, their smooth muscles, Jeremy's shadow of a beard, Michele's curves like every rainbow that had got Joan in trouble, every pot of gold she would always believe in.

One night she lay in her bed and felt her chest, and it was heavy but lighter than the crunch she had felt when giving birth, or when her mother died. In it was a heart that moved like waves, in and out of grief and redemption like the seasons.

One night Darren was sleeping beside her. She couldn't sleep, and his hand twitched, which it often did. She rolled on her side and touched it, knuckles with thin skin, a soft push to her palm pressing it, five knuckles but she could only feel three as he pushed his hand toward the sheet. He sighed and rolled over.

She thought about her children, how they were now in college, how with fortitude they survived online classes, how they were like their own houses, deciding what color to paint every wall they had built or protested. How Michele was a little less of a bitch, and Jeremy wasn't washing his hair much, but at least he cut it.

She felt herself dissolve in the bed and opened her eyes. She turned over and Dexter, lying next to her, started to bark, and one of the cats scratched at the door. She leaned over and touched Dexter's head, and he grew quiet, but she still couldn't sleep. There just seemed to be so much sleep during death. And yet every savior needed to be sacrificed. And to be able to fall into slumber was a kind of holy water.

That night, when she finally did sleep, Joan had a dream. In it, she was young and in a train in Austria. She was leaning against her blue backpack and trying to sleep, and someone said her mother was sleeping in a room above theirs. She would have to climb stairs to a plane. Maneuvering through the middle of a swaying train to the plane, Joan felt a fingernail break against the back of one of the chairs. The chairs were made of blue plastic with cushions patterned in geometric shapes of triangles and squares. Above her the fluorescent lights were piercing. The staircase was across from the restroom.

But then she had to decide if she was willing to fly. If she tried to reach her mother, she would leave the train. She climbed but she was just so tired, a feeling in her marrow, pulsing slowly like blood.

Before she woke up, she was grasping the edge of the floor of the plane and peeking in a room where her parents were both fast asleep, a thin light coming through the round window. She lay on the bed and petted Dexter's wiry fur and thought of the day Filbert died, how they had to put him to sleep during Covid and they all had to wear masks but at least she could look him in the eyes as he faded away. When he was gone, she cried, even though she knew he'd had a long life. She wanted a long life. But she couldn't save anything. She could only help. As she aged, this was what she learned: all you can do is help.

She brushed her palm against the back of Darren's hand, then laid it there and fell back asleep.

The next day Joan made coffee and then went upstairs and took her dinosaur fossil out. She brushed her hand over the rust-colored rock and stared at the outstretched wings with a faint impression of feathers. She kissed it for good luck.

Joan pulled on her purple tennis outfit she had bought, though she didn't play tennis. She loved the dress because it had a pocket for her phone and money, and she was going to a demonstration on 28th street in front of the closed failed businesses of Sports Authority and Walgreens on 28th street. She had announced on Facebook the protest against the speed limit change and felt like she had plenty of support because she had received, in both forums, more than 20 likes.

It was spring and the Principal Officer Engineer and the Neighborhood Speed Management Program had already constructed roads with multiple speed bumps, and soon the speed limit would be reduced to 20 mph. On Quince, they had also installed poles to create one-lane traffic where the cars needed to yield and swerve to drive down the street.

Joan had painted a white sign with *Slow is Not Better!* and drove to the corner. Unfortunately, there was another demonstration at the time regarding the apparent stealing of the elections and the contrition around mask-wearing. Joan parked in the lot and walked toward the demonstration, looking for her tribe. She waded through the crowd, and all the signs were anti-masking signs. One man, with a clean-shaven beard and a crew cut, wearing a gray suit, held a blue sign with *Fear is the Real Virus* written on it. Grizzled and wrinkled as an old peach, a bleached-blond women held a sign that said *Stop Asking Us to Hide* and *Not Breathe.* Joan's eyes roved through the crowd of about twenty people, and not one person was joining her calling.

She came home, fed the pets, cleaned the glass doors leading to the backyard, slept, and woke up angry.

Curdled cream, Dexter's puke on the rug, Darren's sleepy eyes and curly hair rumpled like his foul mood, in disarray with the state of the world in which he still had to work to pay for the kids' colleges, ten more papers for her to grade, the weekend suddenly not a weekend for her at all, Joan decided to drive to a yoga class because Jeremy had told her to do yoga. He said she needed to work on her flexibility. So she slipped on a spandex suit Kate had sold her.

She and Darren sipped coffee in the kitchen. The morning light still fell on a cool day, something they would lose soon, and out the new windows Joan watched two mourning doves fly off their blue spruce.

Darren rubbed his eyes. "What are you doing today?" he asked.

"Yoga and grading," Joan said.

Darren sighed. "I like your suit. Kate has good taste."

Joan smirked.

Kate had sold her the outfit from her sports attire business. "Yes, she does." She thought of the Tarot card she'd pulled that morning of the seven of wands, and how she learned that some battles are really not worth fighting. It was an image of a man dodging flying swords. But she knew she still had battles to fight.

Darren's phone pinged. Her phone pinged.

Michele sent her a text about elephant tusks actually being teeth and how BTW she needed to go to the dentist, and Joan replied as she always did with her kids—the thumbs up sign with a heart.

On her way to yoga, she decided to drive on 26th street where new speed bumps had sprouted everywhere. She observed their construction, how they bled into the bike lane, how now the cyclists would have to enter the road, and bile rose in her throat. She could try to stretch herself into paradise. The world could try to put out fires or drill for natural gas or micromanage addictions or find ways to control every damn move a person made, and the world would not be better for it.

She pushed on the accelerator, then slammed the brakes before each speed bump. At an intersection, she gunned past a stop sign.

In the corners of her eyes blinked a red light that reminded her of fire, and she tasted a familiar taste, like burning mattresses or the taste of forgotten dreams. She glanced at her rearview mirror to see the blinking red lights of a police car.

Acknowledgements

Thank you to these journals that have published some chapters of *As Joan Approaches Infinity*: *Coldnoon, Fiction Southeast, Flash Fiction Magazine,* and *Riot Material.*

My deepest gratitude to the support I had while writing this book. I wrote it within a span of about six years at the same time as I was writing a collection of poetry about postwar Austria and Germany. This pendulum between the two offered me a way to explore two voices that held one subject in common: family, particularly women, in relation to society.

Sarah Elizabeth Schantz and her workshops through *Writes of Passage* and her detailed editing and encouragement of revision helped enormously, and it was through working with Schantz and her community that I gained the confidence that I could write about a character who was deeply flawed. Schantz read the first chaotic draft and helped me establish a timeline and the transitions needed to turn my writing into a novel, along with cutting what didn't serve the book. The feedback from her was invaluable.

Thank you to Toni Oswald and Junior Burke for reading sections of my manuscript and offering feedback and encouragement. Through their thoughtful comments and tips on revision and editing, I was able to create short stories that I painstakingly pieced together into a novel.

I would also like to thank all my friends who supported me on this journey—Staci Bernstein, Claire Ibarra, James Cherry, and Kay Rippy, to name a few. They read my stories and encouraged me to continue. Lys Anzia helped me come up with bizarre scenarios that inspired my imagination, such as Joan and her fears that her children were sniffing glue, the skydiving, and the stealing of an elephant. Thank you also to my swimming friend Betty Kaplan for describing to me the Alcatraz swim and helping me come up with the details to make that chapter as realistic as I could.

Many thanks to Tresha Faye Haefner for her continual support through The Poetry Salon, where during her Saturday generative workshops, I was able to retain my silly and what she calls "bad-ass" voice. That voice, during a pandemic and family situations that were challenging, helped me stay on track to write about Joan.

My deepest gratitude finally and foremost goes out to Heather Goodrich of *Gesture Press* for believing in the project and being willing to publish a book that doesn't fall easily in the category of novel or collection of short stories. Her feedback and willingness to work with me was invaluable and encouraging. I am forever grateful. I am so proud to become part of her press, a publication that prides itself for being radically feminist.

Most of all, thank you to my nuclear family, Michael, Sam, and Eliza for riding my wild waves. Also, deepest gratitude to all the women who are imperfect and striving, who struggle and thrive in a world that so often can be confounding, to the mothers who are redefining gender roles and growing older, embracing adventure and sometimes transcending expectations as well as striving to attain them.

Joan is flawed. She is self-absorbed. Her suburban American world is absurd. She is a disaster in many ways.

However, she is also a version of us, even if our alter ego, a woman who plunges body-first into the world. These are the women who are imperfect, who are fools, who grow not linearly but in the shape of a spiral, whose lives are more waves than crescendos of resolution. This book is for all women, for mothers and the daughters carrying their legacies, for sisters and girlfriends that rocket fearlessly into the future.

Kika Dorsey

is a poet and fiction writer in Boulder, Colorado. She has a PhD in Comparative Literature and her books include the chapbook *Beside Herself* and three full-length collections: *Rust, Coming Up for Air,* and *Occupied: Vienna is a Broken Man* and *Daughter of Hunger,* which won the Colorado Authors' League Award for best poetry collection. She has been nominated for the Pushcart Prize five times.

Currently, she is a lecturer of English at the University of Colorado. Kika also works as a writing coach and ghostwriter. In her free time she swims miles in pools and runs and hikes in the open space of Colorado's mountains and plains.

Made in the USA
Middletown, DE
08 June 2023

32230199R00106